"Julie . . ."
McCoy whispered softly.

He wiped away a tear that had formed at the corner of her eye.

"McCoy."

"Julie, it's wrong to live in constant fear."

"I don't live in fear! It's insane not to listen to an inner warning—"

"Julie," he interrupted her. Moonlight streamed in through the windows. It lit up the silver of his eyes as he spoke. "Julie, I think I love you. But I can't promise to believe."

"Then—"

"But I *can* promise to try," he said softly. He cradled her gently against him. "We can both try. And if we can believe in love again, maybe both of us can believe in life again."

Julie looked up at him. She felt the brush of his thumb against the dampness of her cheek as his lips touched hers.

They would try. . . .

For the moment, it was enough.

Dear Reader,

When two people fall in love, the world is suddenly new and exciting, and it's that same excitement we bring to you in Silhouette Intimate Moments. These are stories with scope and grandeur. The characters lead lives we all dream of, and everything they do reflects the wonder of being in love.

Longer and more sensuous than most romances, Silhouette Intimate Moments novels take you away from everyday life and let you share the magic of love. Adventure, glamour, drama, even suspense—these are the passwords that let you into a world where love has a power beyond the ordinary, where the best authors in the field today create stories of love and commitment that will stay with you always.

In coming months, look for novels by your favorite authors: Kathleen Eagle, Marilyn Pappano, Emilie Richards, Judith Duncan and Justine Davis, to name only a few. And whenever—and wherever—you buy books, look for all the Silhouette Intimate Moments, love stories with that extra something, books written especially for you by today's top authors.

Leslie J. Wainger
Senior Editor and Editorial Coordinator

HEATHER GRAHAM POZZESSERE

SILHOUETTE·INTIMATE·MOMENTS®

Published by Silhouette Books New York

America's Publisher of Contemporary Romance

SILHOUETTE BOOKS
300 East 42nd St., New York, N.Y. 10017

HATFIELD AND McCOY

ISBN: 0-373-07416-6

First Silhouette Books printing January 1992

Printed in the U.S.A.

Books by Heather Graham Pozzessere

Silhouette Intimate Moments

Night Moves #118
The di Medici Bride #132
Double Entendre #145
The Game of Love #165
A Matter of Circumstance #174
Bride of the Tiger #192
All in the Family #205
King of the Castle #220
Strangers in Paradise #225
Angel of Mercy #248
This Rough Magic #260
Lucia in Love #265
Borrowed Angel #293
A Perilous Eden #328
Forever My Love #340
Wedding Bell Blues #352
Snowfire #386
Hatfield and McCoy #416

Silhouette Books

Silhouette Christmas Stories 1991
"The Christmas Bride"

HEATHER GRAHAM POZZESSERE

considers herself lucky to live in Florida, where she can indulge her love of water sports, like swimming and boating, year-round. Her background includes stints as a model, actress and bartender. She was once actually tied to the railroad tracks to garner publicity for the dinner theater where she was acting. Now she's a full-time wife, mother of five and, of course, a writer of historical and contemporary romances.

Prologue

The dream came to her again that night, and she smiled in her sleep. It was a sweet dream, and she welcomed it as she would a lover.

Ah, but it was a dream that brought her a lover and warmth and soft, sensual pleasure.

She never saw his face. She was always looking out the window, looking at the rich grasses and beautiful blues and greens of summer...or perhaps it was spring. There was always a light breeze. The kind of breeze that just lightly lifted her hair.

And then she would know that he was in the room.

She would know...

Because of a subtle, masculine scent. She would know because she would feel him there.

And the warmth and tenderness would fill her. She knew him, knew the man, and knew things about him that made her love him. She didn't need to see his face.

Didn't need to know the color of his eyes, or the color of his hair.

She knew all the hues within his heart and soul and mind, and those colors were all beautiful and part of the warmth that touched her.

He could move so silently...

He would be coming across the room to her, and she would know it, and she would smile. She would know that he was coming closer, because she could always feel him near. Feel the security, the supreme sense of well-being, that came to her when she was with him.

Her lover...

Tonight...

He stood behind her and swept the fall of her hair from her neck, and she felt the wet, hot caress of his lips against her nape.

The pleasure was startling. So startling that a certain embarrassment touched her in her sleep, nearly ending the dream.

But her sleep was deep, and her enchantment was even deeper.

He held back her hair, and his kiss skimmed over her shoulder. She wore something that hugged her body. Something dark. He lifted the strap from her shoulder. Even the feel of the fabric leaving her skin was erotic.

By his touch, by his command, the garment fell from her shoulders. Bit by bit, the clothing was peeled from her body. And bit by bit it fell away to the ground, in a pool of darkness at her feet.

His arms encircled her. She could feel the strength of his naked chest as he pulled her against him. He still wore jeans. She could feel the roughness of the fabric against the tender skin of her bare flanks. Even that touch was sensual.

So vividly sensual. Even in a dream.

And she knew that she dreamed...

His whisper touched her ear. She could not hear the words, but a lazy smile came to her lips. Then she was turning against him.

She didn't see his face.

She felt his kiss.

Felt the hungry pressure of his lips, forming over her own, firmly, demandingly, causing them to part for the exotic presence of his tongue.

He'd kissed her before...

Never quite like this.

And when his lips left her mouth, they touched her throat. Touched the length of it. The soft, slow, sensual stroke of his tongue just brushing her flesh. With ripples of silken, liquid fire. She could see his hands, broad, so darkly tanned, on the paleness of her skin. His fingers were long, handsomely tapered, calloused, but with neatly clipped nails. Masculine hands. Hands that touched with an exciting expertise. Fingers that stroked with confidence and pleasure.

She allowed her head to fall back, her eyes to close. The sensations to surround her.

The breeze...it was so cool against her naked body. So soft. So unerringly sensual. Perhaps because her body was so hot. Growing fevered. But the air...it touched her where his kiss left off, and both fire and ice seemed to come to her and dance through her.

She spun in his arms. It was no longer daytime. Shadows were falling, and the breeze was growing cooler.

And his kiss went lower.

And where his lips touched her, she burned.

And where his lips had lingered earlier, the cool air stroked her with a sensuality all its own.

She dreamed, she tried to tell herself.

It was not real.

But within her dream lover's arms, his kiss lowered. And lowered until he teased the base of her spine. His hand caressed her naked buttocks and hips, and she was turning in his arms.

Her hand rested on his head, her breath quickened and caught, and quickened again. She cried out, amazed at the tempest that rose within her, startled by the sheer sensual pleasure that ripped through her.

She cried out again and again, and then discovered that she was sinking, sinking into his arms...

Night had come. The moon remained in the sky, but she could not see clearly.

She still did not see his face. She could touch and feel, but she could not see his face.

Not that she was thinking. Not even in the dream could she reason or think, for she was with him, touching him, knowing the living warmth and fire of him. Feeling the ripple of muscle in his chest. Feeling his hands. Feeling the pulse of his body. Feeling...him.

It was vivid. So vivid.

She could feel him entering her...

She began to fight the dream. It was too vivid. It was decadent...

Even in the privacy of sleep, it was embarrassing.

And still, she knew what went on. She knew the moment in the dream when the stars burst and the sky seemed to turn a glorious gold, and then to blacken again.

She knew the absolute amazement she felt at the force of the love they shared. She knew the shattering pounding of her heart, the desperate scramble to breathe again, the sheen of perspiration that bathed them both like a lover's dew....

For it was sweet, all so very sweet. He would envelop her in his arms. She would lie upon his shoulder and feel that incredible security and the simple pleasure of being together. She would reach out and hold him and she knew that she would see his face...

But the tenderness did not come, nor did the overwhelming feeling of well-being.

A different feeling had been coming on...coming on for long, long moments.

Then it seized her. Seized her firmly. Darkness. A startling, terrifying darkness. A presence. Near them.

And she cried out.

What is it?

She heard his whisper. She tried to talk. She was choking, and she was so frightened. Her jaw was locked. Constricted. She fought so hard.

He's here! He can see us!

No...

Oh, my God! He's trying to watch us.

No, he cannot watch us.

But the feeling wouldn't leave her. She closed her eyes, tightly. Still, there suddenly seemed to be a light. A blinding light.

She saw a man's shoulder. Fleetingly, in that light. A bronzed shoulder. There was a short but jagged scar on it.

The light faded. She couldn't see anything.

She was disoriented. Confused. Frightened.

Had she seen her lover's shoulder...?

Or had it been his? The man who watched. The one who so terrified her...

Julie...

Her lover whispered to her. He tried to reassure her. He was confident in his own strength. He didn't believe. He didn't understand.

It was so frightening. Did the scar belong to a man who would hold her against all danger?

Or did it belong to a cold-blooded killer?

Julie! Julie, please...

I'm afraid, she told him. She didn't say it out loud. And he denied any sixth sense.

But this time, he had heard her.

I'm with you.

She strained. Strained against the darkness. If only she could see his face, it would be all right. If she could just see her lover's face...

But there was too much darkness. She couldn't see.

And the terror was beginning to suffocate her. She couldn't breathe.

The darkness was coming closer and closer.

She awoke with a start and realized she was screaming.

"Oh!"

With a gasp, she turned on her bedside lamp. She was still shaking. She was drenched with perspiration.

She looked around the room. Nothing had changed. She was home, safe on her mountain.

"What a dream!" she murmured.

She rose, still hot and flushed, and walked into the kitchen for a long drink of water, then returned to bed. She smiled sheepishly. "I wonder if that was a defense mechanism against this dream lover of mine," she rationalized aloud. "Oh, but a shrink would have a heyday with me!"

She grinned and laid her head down. The fear was gone. Completely gone. It was incredibly easy to close her eyes and sleep again.

No more dreams taunted her. When she awoke in the morning, she had forgotten just how frightened she had been. She speculated about the dream man as she showered, grinning, wondering if she would ever meet the man. If she would stand in the breeze, and feel his caress...

She groaned aloud. Patty would blame her life-style, she was certain. Too secluded.

And so, so often, when she dreamed...

She flushed.

Maybe she would meet him.

For just a moment, she felt a tinge of fear. As if the darkness was coming over her again.

But then it was gone. She gave herself a firm mental shake.

And she started to wonder again. About him.

She showered, dressed and made herself a cup of tea and an English muffin. She speculated once again about her mystery lover as she curled up on the huge chair on the porch that overlooked both mountain and valley. She felt wonderfully at ease.

And it was then that the phone began to ring.

Chapter 1

They were destined to come together and to clash.

But that first time Julie saw the man—for all her intuitive powers—she had no idea that she would ever see him again.

Nor did she want to!

She was in a hurry. Admittedly, she was very much in a hurry. But when she rounded the corner in her little Mazda, she was certain that she had the right of way. She hadn't even seen the Lincoln that came around from the opposite side at exactly the same time.

And so they rammed, head first, right into one another.

Luckily, they were both going five miles an hour, and both cars had huge, brand-new bumpers.

They collided and bounced.

Shaken, Julie realized that they had been really lucky. They had struck one another just as if they had been playing bumper cars. There was no damage to her car, and she was certain that there was no damage to the heavier Lincoln.

She could drive away. Thank God. She couldn't afford the time to exchange insurance information or wait around to make a police report.

The other car started to back away. She sighed with relief. She revved her car and backed away from the Lincoln. Then she paused politely.

But the other driver was pausing, too.

They both paused.

And paused.

Julie squinted, trying to see the driver. It was a man, she discerned. And he was letting her go first.

He gave a short bump to his horn.

She started at the sound, then jerked forward.

He eased forward, too.

Once again, they slammed together.

They were playing bumper cars. Julie smiled.

She started to wave at the driver in the Lincoln. But watching him, she felt her smile begin to freeze.

He wasn't smiling. Nor was he going to drive away this time.

He was getting out of his car and coming her way.

He was wearing black jeans, a black leather jacket and dark sunglasses. He was somewhere between thirty and forty—big, tall, broad-shouldered, but lean and graceful in his movements.

And he reached her window quickly. Damned quickly.

"Are you hurt?" he demanded.

"No," she said quickly. "No, I'm not hurt."

"Are you sure? Absolutely sure?"

Her smile came to life again. He seemed concerned, honestly concerned. And he had such a deep, rich, masculine voice. She didn't just hear his voice; she felt it. With all of her body. It left a pleasant, shivery warmth inside her.

He had a nice, clean-shaven jawline—a strong one. And a nice mouth. Full, broad. Warm and sensual.

He might have been the man in her dreams, she thought. Before the darkness had descended. The darkness that even now threatened an uneasy feeling.

"I'm not hurt at all," she assured him quickly.

And then his tone changed. Boy, did it change.

"What the hell did you think you were doing!" he grated out. Now his voice was full of authority and command.

It instantly struck a chord within her.

"Me! What the hell did you think you were doing?"

"You little pea brain, I had the clear cut right-of-way. I even tried to let you go first. Given the fact that you're driving with your head in the clouds, your talent for accidents makes sense."

Pea brain? No, this was not the man in her dream. Definitely not!

"Excuse me, sir," she purred sweetly, her lashes lowering over her eyes. Fight fire with oil, that's what she'd always heard. "But you did not have any right-of-way, and I'm afraid that you do seem to be in a black-leathered mental wasteland. There's no reason—"

"I was clearly—"

"You most certainly were not—" Julie interrupted. But she didn't faze him. And she didn't have a chance to explain to him that the right-of-way had been entirely hers.

"Not the one required to yield." He finished his sentence, then looked at her, the slightest curve touching his lip. "Black-leathered mental wasteland?" he repeated, astounded that she should say such a thing.

"I am not a pea brain," she said with incredible dignity.

He might have almost smiled then, but he didn't. That jaw of his squared right away.

"Never mind!" He waved a hand dismissively in the air. "I don't have the time for a petty argument. Be glad." He waged a warning finger at her. "You'd get points on your license for a moving violation."

Of all the incredible effrontery. She stared at him for a moment, then she wanted to scream. No, she wanted to jump out of the car and wag a finger at him—all the way back to that big Lincoln of his. What she really wanted was to give him a sound slap on his arrogant cheekbone. She gritted her teeth. Foolish. She couldn't see his eyes, she couldn't really see his face. She could see that he stood well over six feet tall. The better part of valor warned her to stay seated. And to smile.

"I'm quite sure you would receive points on your license, sir, for this violation. Fortunately for you, I'm in far too much of a hurry to squander time on the petty pursuit of proving a point. Now, if you'll excuse me . . ."

She didn't wait for a reply. She backed smoothly, then gunned the gas pedal as she hadn't done since she'd been a sophomore in high school, just learning to drive.

And then she couldn't help but smile with pure, sweet satisfaction.

Hmm. Spiteful, Julie, she warned herself. But she just couldn't help the feeling of victory and pleasure. He'd been so rude. So arrogant. He'd barely managed to keep his mouth shut about the fact that she was a woman driver.

It would have been one of his next lines, she was certain.

Still, she chided herself, you almost ran over his toes.

"Almost. But I didn't," she said aloud. "Well, he did have to step back rather quickly. But that's what he gets for being such an orangutan."

She maneuvered her small car around another curve and then saw the police station not far before her. Her smile faded. She remembered why she had been in such a hurry.

Time was so very important.

She pulled in and parked her car. She had barely opened the front door to the station, walked in and started to close the door before it was nearly ripped out of her hands. She let go of the door and stepped back.

A gasp of amazement escaped her.

It was the man. The tall blond man in the black leather who had been driving the big Lincoln.

Lord! He'd come after her, she thought in a moment of panic. She almost jumped back. He'd come after her to do her some harm for nearly running over his toes.

She was in a police station, for God's sake! she reminded herself. She couldn't possibly be in any danger here.

"Where's Petty?" he demanded of the two officers on duty, one man and one young woman.

Petty was the chief. Chief Pettigrew. Only people who knew him well called him Petty.

The man was quick to take in the office. All of the office. And his gaze, beneath the dark glasses, came down hard upon Julie.

He pulled off the sunglasses and glared at her. He wasn't smiling. There wasn't the faintest trace of amusement about him. One brow shot up, then his face creased into a deep frown. He turned to the two officers at the front desk.

"Where's Petty?" he said again.

The male officer jumped to his feet. "Right this way, sir. He's expecting you. If you'll follow me—"

But the man shot Julie another hard look. One that seemed to sizzle and burn her from head to toe. Then he burst into the chief's office—with the officer following behind. A door slammed in his wake.

Staring after him, Julie lifted her chin. She took a few steps forward and sat in the plain brown chair before the desk of the remaining officer, Patty Barnes.

"Oh, no!" Julie breathed. Her abilities had certainly been failing her so far this morning. She was only now coming to see the absolutely obvious, and it was not good at all. "Oh, no..."

"What?" Patty whispered.

"Please tell me that that man isn't..."

Patty stared at her.

"Patty, he can't be!"

"But he is," Patty said.

"He's the G-man?"

"That's him," Patty replied. "The G-man."

Julie didn't get a chance to speak again. Sound suddenly seemed to burst upon them.

"What?"

Hearing the single word explode in the FBI agent's decidedly masculine voice, Julie winced.

Apparently, he wasn't very happy, either. He'd already heard about her, she realized. And he must have put two and two together and realized that she was the woman with whom he would be working.

"What?" Again he said the word. It wasn't a question. She was tempted to leap up and go striding into the chief's office.

Curiously, she was able to grant that he was an attractive man, despite his awful arrogance.

It had only been seconds that she had really seen him with those dark glasses removed. And in that little bit of time before he had crossed into the inner offices, his eyes had touched upon her.

They went well with his jaw.

They were steel-gray eyes. Eyes as hard and rigid as the structure beams for a skyscraper, eyes that were truly gray, without a hint of blue. He had sandy blond close-cropped hair, a bronzed face with rugged, well-defined features, and curiously dark lashes and brows for the blondness of his hair.

All in all, the combinations and contrasts created a very interesting face. And the face went well with the tall, taut, well-muscled body that could move with such startling ease and grace for its size. She'd barely heard his footsteps, but then she'd really only been aware of his eyes, those steel-gray eyes with their dark, probing ability.

Suddenly his voice exploded again. "I don't believe this! You want me to work with a witch of some sort? Me? Of all people. A voodoo priestess? That—that child out there!"

Smile tiger, smile! she ordered herself. And she did so, grinning to Patty. "I really don't think he's pleased," Julie murmured.

Thirty-year-old Patty had a pleasantly pretty freckled face and light red hair that was swept up in a ponytail. She arched a brow at Julie's words.

"No, I don't think so, either," she murmured.

Julie gritted her teeth. She'd come across the attitude often enough, and it barely disturbed her anymore. She'd controlled her temper, and she'd made herself credible by being entirely calm and dignified. It had been a long time since anyone had managed to make her feel quite so angry.

"Arrogant bastard," she said softly to Patty.

"Oh, he's really not that bad," Patty said quickly.

It was Julie's turn to arch a brow.

"Well, all right," Patty responded. "He is a toughie. I really had no idea who the bureau was sending, but, yes, he is going to be tough. But the man is good, Julie. And he can be a real heartthrob when he wants. He sometimes has a smile that could melt rock, I swear it. And he's good, Julie, so good. Thorough. So he growls a bit. When he isn't growling—"

"He's probably trying to bite," Julie interrupted.

Patty laughed. "Okay, so he's hardheaded and—"

"Ruthless?" Julie suggested.

"Well, there's sort of a deep, dark mystery about the man, too. He's originally from this area, but apparently he spent about ten years out in California. Something happened out there. I don't know what it was. No one does. He doesn't talk about himself."

"No," Julie said. "He doesn't talk at all. He just barks."

"But still," Patty said with a sigh, "there's something about him . . . I admit, my ticker has gone pitter-patter often enough over Robert—"

"No! It's absolutely out of the question!" Good old heartthrob Robert was spewing again.

A quieter voice of reason must have spoken in the inner offices against the man's tirade, but that voice of reason was apparently getting nowhere. The man's argument was rising again, and Patty's cheeks grew red as she stared at Julie. The man must know that he was being heard very clearly—by everyone.

"It's not out of the question!" Julie said firmly, her unsolicited reply in the outer office just as quiet as the man's statement in the inner office had been forceful.

"Not out of the question at all," Julie continued, flashing a smile at Patty. "I was asked in. I'm staying. Even if it upsets Mr. Robert—" She broke off, looking at Patty with a frown. "What's his name?"

Patty opened her mouth to speak, then quickly paused. A long, "Oh!" escaped her.

Julie stared at her blankly. "His name is Robert Oh?"

"Oh! No, I mean, no, of course not," Patty said quickly. "It's just that . . ."

"Well, what?" Julie tapped her long nails against the leather of her handbag.

Patty suddenly smiled, then laughed. "His name is McCoy. Robert McCoy."

"Oh!" Julie said. And then her mouth curled into a smile, and she was laughing, too. "Well, maybe that just figures. Mr. Robert McCoy..." Her voice trailed away, then she added, "If he's looking for a feud, Patty, he's going to get one. I'm needed on this case, I know it, I feel it. And I'm here to stay."

The deep, thundering burst of a bald expletive came from the inner office. The hostility and anger behind it were enough to make Patty feel as if her red hair were standing on end at the base of her neck.

But Julie Hatfield was undaunted. Small, delicate, with a fine, beautiful bone structure and the sweet face of an angel, she sat straight on her chair. She was almost regal with her sun-blond hair caught back from her face and swept into an elegant French braid. She appeared not to have heard Robert McCoy at all.

But then Julie's eyes touched Patty's. Hazel eyes, they had the ability to glisten like gold. And they were glistening now.

Patty smiled. Perhaps Mr. Robert McCoy did need to watch out this time around.

Miss Hatfield was ready to do battle.

Inside the chief's office, Robert McCoy was prepared to go to war.

He stared hard from Chief Pettigrew to his sergeant, Timothy Riker, still unable to believe what he had just heard.

Timothy Riker, obviously dazed that he was between the chief and McCoy, looked up as a dark red flush stained his features. Robert was sorry to see

Riker so uncomfortable—he was a good man, young and dedicated, but he should have known that what was going on would touch off Robert's temper.

It was all entirely unacceptable.

Timothy cleared his throat. He was loyal to the death, trying to help out Petty.

"Lieutenant McCoy—" Riker broke off. Steel-gray eyes were fixed mercilessly on him. Thankfully, the chief broke in.

"Robert, these orders aren't from me, and they aren't from any of the local police stations involved. They came direct from your own office. Now, I do admit that we've worked with—"

"This quack!" Robert McCoy said flatly.

"She's not a quack, honest, sir!" Riker piped. Then he was flushing again.

Curious, Robert decided. It was obvious that Riker was fond of the woman, whoever she was. This Julie something. Ah, but that, my young man, Robert thought, is because of your very youth! A pretty face, a soft word...

He fought to control his temper. If time wasn't entirely of the essence, he might even have been amused, intrigued.

No, he couldn't be amused. Or intrigued. He'd met others like this woman before.

He inhaled. Exhaled. That was the past. A closed door. He was going to be coolly amused. And more.

Determined, even, to unmask this so-called psychic.

And a child's life was involved.

He was good, a damned good investigative agent, and he knew it. His work was his life. He could find clues few other men would seek, and during the instances when he had been in direct contact with a kidnapper, he had been somewhat startled to realize that many of his long-ago psychology classes had paid off—he was capable of setting up a communication that could save a life.

Maybe it wasn't the psychology classes. Maybe it had just been life itself.

Life was often a wicked, wicked teacher.

None of that really mattered now. There were numerous local police stations involved in this region where the states of Virginia, West Virginia and Maryland came together in a grand cataclysm of nature. But he was the federal agent, and the man put in charge. Not that he was so much of a loner—he could work well with others. He had to. So many experts were needed, men who could comb woods, technicians who could magically read minute drops of blood and come up with incredible information. He needed others. Men and women who had some sense and could work with logic.

Not some kind of a mystic quack!

Chief Pettigrew, a man with bright blue eyes, graying hair, a salt and pepper beard and the look of a department-store Santa, sighed softly and tried once again. "Robert, give the girl a chance, eh? She's been a tremendous help in other cases."

Robert McCoy was startled when his fist landed against the desk. "Time, Petty," he said. "Time! There's a little girl missing, Petty, an eight-year-old child. We just don't have time to bring in a soothsayer!"

Time had been important to him once before.

Pettigrew stood, then sank back in his chair. Robert McCoy wasn't a stranger called in to take charge of one of his cases. Robert was the son of one of Pettigrew's oldest and dearest friends.

He wasn't going to be intimidated by the son of a friend, he assured himself.

It was just that, well, McCoy was an intimidating man. Maybe he even had the right to be so furious about this call. And despite this dark display of temper, he was a damned good man, too, Petty knew, from past experience. McCoy was passionate about his work. And he was smart, smart as a whip. He'd studied criminal law in school and he had proven time and time again his ability to analyze the mind of a criminal. He could be a hard man, almost ruthless in the pursuit of his objectives.

Especially since California. No matter how hard a man he appeared to be. No matter how silent. He had changed. And he was capable of being ruthless.

But that was exactly why he had been called in on this case. A child's life was at stake.

Of course, it was exactly why Julie Hatfield had been called in on the case, too.

"Robert!" Pettigrew leaned toward his towering blond friend. "We have nothing on this case. Nothing at all. We know that the girl disappeared from her own street, and that's all we've got. That and the suspicion—" He broke off. They all knew what the suspicion was. There had been a similar case in a neighboring county not six months ago. A young woman had been abducted from her home. A ransom letter had come, and a ransom had been delivered. But the woman had not been returned.

Julie Hatfield had been called in on that case. And she had found the young woman, barely in time, buried, but alive, in an old refrigerator upon the mountaintop.

Six months before that, there had been another similar case. The young woman taken during that abduction had never been found.

The kidnapper, assuming it was one and the same man—or woman—had struck again and was moving between state lines. And that was why Robert had been called in.

"Robert," Pettigrew said wearily. "We need Julie on this one. She can help. You just don't know her."

McCoy ran his fingers through his hair and sank into an office chair beside Timothy Riker. Why was he so furious? Because working with this girl could take time? Yes, of course. He was also bone weary. He'd just returned from a sting in Florida, and he'd thought he'd have some time off. It was moving into late spring. The fish were jumping. His own little mountaintop was beckoning to him, and for the first time in a long time, he wanted some time off.

And he was scared, too. He was always scared, though he never let it show. Dear Lord, it was always scary to hold someone's life in your hands. And now, it was a child's life, and more. The lives of her parents, her family, her friends. If she was lost forever, they would be, too. No one ever forgot the loss of a loved one. Ever.

Ever.

And he was mad, of course, that anyone could claim the things that the charlatan in the front office was pretending she could do.

It could lead to nothing but false hope.

Maybe worse.

No one but God could see into the hearts and minds of other men. No one could see the pathetic remnants of a case gone bad except for those poor investigators sent out to retrieve the body.

"It came down to us straight from the top, Robert. They say that we must use her on this one," Pettigrew said very softly.

Robert McCoy rubbed his temple with his thumb and forefinger.

"How many hours now since the little girl was taken?"

"Three," Timothy Riker informed him quickly. "And we've had men and women out scouring the neighboring woods since the call came in."

"Three hours," Robert mused. He glanced quickly at the chief. "And there's no possibility that she just ran off with friends? That she saw something interesting—"

"No, none at all. Tracy Nicholson is a very conscientious little girl. She never strayed at all. She would have never worried her mother so."

This had to be murder for old Petty, Robert thought, and he was sorry again for his outburst of temper. This was a small town, and Petty was friends with little Tracy's parents, and with Tracy herself.

"Signs of a struggle?" Robert said. He had to ask.

Riker nodded. "Scuffs in the dirt right off the road. She was definitely taken, sir."

"We've had men combing the woods since."

Good and bad. If the little girl was near, she'd be found. And if not, well, valuable clues might have been trampled into oblivion.

Riker cleared his throat again. "The child's parents are waiting at their home."

Good Lord, he was wasting time here, McCoy realized unhappily. Damn.

Swallow that temper, he warned himself, and swallow the past. It had all been so long ago now. So long. Still, it was hard.

Hard when he knew his psychic was the soft and delicate blonde in the outer office. That dear, sweet young woman with the angelic face...

And whiplash tongue.

And wretched driving skills, to boot.

"McCoy, I swear to you," Petty said, "the orders did come straight from the top—"

"Yes, yes, fine. Riker is right. Let's get moving. Take me out to meet Miss What's-her-name."

Petty, who had started to lead the way out of his office, paused suddenly and swung back. And despite the circumstances, he was grinning.

"It's Hatfield."

"Pardon?" McCoy said.

"Her name." Petty's rheumy blue gaze surveyed him with a certain amusement. "Darned if I didn't just realize it all myself. Hatfield. Her name is Julie Hatfield. Hell, McCoy, this isn't your feud. The Hatfields and McCoys have been at it for decades, eh?"

Hatfield. Her name was Hatfield.

Hell, after everything else today, it just figured.

He crunched his jaw into the most affable grin he could manage. Only his eyes were steam.

"Excuse me, Petty."

He brushed past the old chief, letting the glass-paned door slam behind him as he strode quickly through the outer office.

She saw him coming. She stood quickly.

She was something. Petite, blond...cute. No, actually, she was beautiful. Her features were so fine, so perfectly chiseled. She was elegant. Even in jeans and a light knit sweater. And sneakers. There was still something elegant about her.

And those eyes of hers. Almost golden. With such a wicked, wicked gleam.

Two could play...And two could feud.

She was smiling. A smile plastered into place, of course.

His own grin could have been rubber.

"Well, well, so we meet again," he said softly.

Don't you dare think that you've won anything! he warned in silence, offering her his hand. She accepted it. His fingers curled over hers.

"Yes, so we meet again," she told him politely.

And somehow, he sensed her silent reply.

I did win the first battle, McCoy!

His fingers tightened around hers. They were both still smiling.

And old Petty was beaming away, thinking that his team was together at last.

Subtly, McCoy pulled her a shade closer. His words were light. In jest. "So it's to be Hatfield versus McCoy, eh?" he murmured.

Her lashes, luxurious, long and honey dark, swept her cheeks. And her gaze was regal and sweet when her eyes met his again. All innocence.

"Oh, no, sir. It's to be Hatfield *and* McCoy, I believe."

Hatfield and McCoy...

His grin was suddenly real.

It just wasn't meant to be.

Chapter 2

They left the station together, and as soon as they were outside, he headed toward his car. She quickly stated that she didn't mind driving, but the force of his stride had her at the passenger door to his car before she could even complete the words. There was an incredibly firm touch to his hands as he—courteously?—helped her into the car, and an unshakable firmness to his quick, curt words. "I'll drive."

If he wanted an obedient silence from her, he wasn't going to get it. He might think she was a quack, but she'd come up against the attitude before. He might be as aggressive as a tiger when he chose, but she knew how to fight back.

Politely.

"Do you know where the house is?" she asked.

"I have the address, yes, thank you."

"But do you know where the house is? The streets around here curve."

He glanced her way with his teeth nearly bared. "I know where I'm going!"

She simply wasn't going to be intimidated.

This was a matter of life and death. They had to get along. And he had to learn that he had to listen to her.

She leaned back. "Go straight down the road here, then make a left. It should be the third or fourth house in."

He glanced her way again. There was a steel sizzle to his eyes. It was electric. She nearly jumped from the power of that gaze.

But she didn't. She'd never let him know that he managed to nonplus her.

Maybe his eyes shot silver bullets, but he didn't ignore her directions. He turned the black Lincoln just as she had directed.

There was no mistaking the house. As soon as they came around the corner, Julie saw the kidnapped little girl's parents waiting. There were other people around them. Family, friends, perhaps. The Nicholsons, she thought quickly, remembering everything she had been told. Martin and Louisa. And their little girl's name was Tracy. She would be eight next week.

The lawn, the neighborhood looked so normal, so peaceful. It was spring, and Louisa Nicholson had planted all kinds of flowers along the walkway. The house was freshly painted a bright white with green trim around the windows and doors. It was a moderately affluent neighborhood, a working neighborhood, a place where *Sesame Street* and Disney movies would play for the children, where hope blossomed for the best of lives, where the American dream could be played out.

But not today.

Robert McCoy pulled his Lincoln to the side of the road. The engine was still revving down when Julie opened her door and hurried out. She smiled reassuringly as she walked up the steps to the cement pathway leading to the broad porch and the house. She knew the girl's mother instantly—a small woman with dark curly hair and large brown eyes that kept filling with tears. She stood beside a lean man with thinning gray-black hair. "Mr. Nicholson?" She shook his hand, then turned quickly to his wife. "Mrs. Nicholson? I'm Julie Hatfield. Petty sent me from his office, and a Mr. McCoy, FBI, is right behind me. You mustn't worry, really. I don't know what Petty told you about me, but I am very good, and I'm certain that at this moment, Tracy is fine. Just fine."

Something in her words must have reached Mrs. Nicholson because some of the cloud seemed to disappear from her eyes. She smiled at Julie, then looked over Julie's shoulder. McCoy was coming toward them.

"Mrs. Nicholson, I'm—" he began.

"Yes, yes, you're the FBI man," Louisa Nicholson said. "Julie, please come in. My husband and I will help you in any way we can. Oh, Mr.—did you say McCoy, Miss Hatfield?"

They were going to go through a lot of this, Julie thought.

She smiled. "Yes, he's a McCoy. Isn't it just disgraceful?"

"Miss Hatfield—" McCoy began, that deep voice filled with all kinds of authority.

It didn't matter. Louisa Nicholson actually laughed, and her tall, balding husband at her side almost grinned.

"We're just so very worried," Martin Nicholson said.

"Naturally," Julie said softly. "Shall we go in?"

The Nicholsons excused themselves to the anxious friends and neighbors who had gathered around. Julie saw a few friends from church and waved, then hurriedly followed the Nicholsons into the parlor. Julie glanced around quickly. It was a warm house. A house, she thought, where a lot of love lived. There was a beautiful china cabinet to one side of the entry, filled with various collections of crystal and figurines. The two hutches that filled out the parlor were mahogany, rich and beautifully polished. But the sofa and chairs in the center of the room were overstuffed and very comfortable. A little girl could crawl all over them without worrying about being yelled at. She could curl into her father's lap there, rest her head against her mother's shoulder.

Robert McCoy had begun an intense round of questioning. Julie could tell that the Nicholsons had already been through it all; their answers were becoming mechanical.

The Nicholsons knew that Tracy hadn't run away. She was a good girl, she loved them both, she was an only child, and they were a very close family. She had been right out front, and then suddenly she had been gone. All the wonderful people out in the yard had searched the house, the lawn and the streets beyond, and they had even organized block searches. The police had come by, and now Mr. McCoy and Julie Hatfield were here.

Julie was surprised to find herself distracted momentarily as she watched McCoy. He had the ability to be kind, to be gentle. He spoke to the Nicholsons with a depth and understanding that startled Julie.

She had thought him all business, cut and dried. But there was a heart pumping in that broad chest.

He was a very handsome man. Those steel-gray eyes were direct and powerful in a handsome face that was strongly, ruggedly sculpted.

He probably chews nails for dinner, Julie thought.

He didn't really look like a G-man, not in that black leather jacket of his. G-men were supposed to wear three-piece suits.

Maybe he did wear suits on occasion. He would be just as tall in a suit. His shoulders would be every bit as broad. Maybe he'd be even more intimidating.

He wasn't intimidating. Yes, he was. But he did have a heart in that rock-hard chest, she had determined. Either that, or he was just so professional that he could make his voice sound as if he were caring.

Something suddenly flashed briefly through her mind.

He cared too much. That was it. He cared too much. He took every case right to his heart...

Julie turned toward the window and started. They were still talking behind her. Suddenly, she could see what had happened. She could see it all.

There was Tracy Nicholson. She was a tall girl for seven, maybe four feet three inches. And she didn't look a thing like her parents. She had bright red hair and a cute spattering of freckles across her nose. She was wearing nearly brand new blue jeans and a white blouse with a Peter Pan collar and a pretty navy sweater. She had been rolling a ball down the steps. The ball had rolled out into the street. It was then that the car...

The car. She couldn't quite see the car. All Julie knew was that it was some kind of a sedan, and not a compact car. And it seemed to be a darkish color. It drew near the curb.

The driver was calling to Tracy.

Julie inhaled and exhaled slowly. She could feel her heart thundering, just as Tracy had felt her little heart pound ferociously.

Tracy had been taught by her parents never to get into a car with a stranger. She had been taught to be polite, but careful.

And now there was this someone...

Julie tried to see into the mist surrounding the car and driver. She couldn't. She just couldn't.

Not even when the driver swore because Tracy would come no closer. Swore, and leaped quickly out of the seat, rushing for Tracy.

Tracy tried to scream, tried to run. She could do neither. Julie could feel the little girl's terror. Her feet had felt like cement. She couldn't budge them. And her scream...her scream had caught in her throat. And just when it might have burst out, something was clamped tightly over her mouth. Something with an awful, strong odor. Tracy tried to fight then. She tried very hard, and her shoes dug into the dirt. But that stuff on the cloth made it harder and harder to move.

She couldn't even think anymore. It was something awful. Something that stole the light . . .

It was gone. A flash of blackness appeared before Julie's eyes, and she knew. The little girl had lost consciousness then.

". . . white shirt, and jeans," Louisa Nicholson was saying. "And her high-top sneakers."

"And her navy blue sweater," Julie said softly.

"What?" Louisa said.

Julie turned around. "She was wearing her navy sweater," she said.

Martin Nicholson gasped softly. "That's right, Louisa, she was. She told me she was going to get her sweater while I was fixing the pipe out back. She ran in and put it on. I'd clear forgotten until now. We gave the other officers the wrong description of her clothing—"

"It doesn't matter," Julie said quickly. "What matters now is that we get her back." She glanced at Robert. He was watching her carefully, his eyes narrowed. But he didn't try to shut her up. He was unimpressed with her knowledge about the sweater, certainly, but he didn't seem to mind her presence so much anymore.

"There were originally scuff marks in the dirt on the shoulder of the road?" McCoy asked quietly. He didn't say it reproachfully, and he didn't let on that valuable clues might have been gained had the dirt and grass and the shoulder not been so trampled. It was a foolish waste, but it wouldn't do any good to tell the Nicholsons now.

Louisa nodded and sniffed, then suddenly the tears she had been trying to hold back came streaming down her cheeks. "She fought him. My baby fought him. He must have hurt her, oh, how he must have hurt her—"

"No, no, Louisa!" Julie said quickly. She sat beside Louisa on the plush old comfortable couch, taking the woman into her arms. "No, please, trust me, believe in me. Yes, Tracy was frightened, and she did fight. She's a wonderfully tough little girl, and the two of you have taught her to be so resourceful. But he hasn't hurt her. He's going to ask for a ransom. He wants money, not to hurt anyone. You wait and see. It's all going to come out all right."

"The phone line has been tapped?" McCoy said.

Martin Nicholson nodded. "The police did that right away. Petty told us there would be a man listening in every time our phone rings and that if a ransom demand came, they'd try to trace the line immediately."

"That's good. That's real good," McCoy said. "Well, I think we'd better get started on what we have."

"Officer Smith is still out searching the woods around the house with some volunteers," Martin Nicholson said.

"Fine," McCoy said. "Have you got a picture of Tracy for me?" he asked.

Louisa leaped to her feet and hurried out of the room. She returned quickly with an eight-by-ten photograph in a bronze frame, handing it to McCoy.

"May I keep this for now?" he asked.

"Of course."

"Stand by your phone," McCoy said, shaking Louisa's hand, then her husband's. "We'll do everything in our power."

He started out. Julie lingered, shaking Martin's hand, too, and impulsively giving Louisa a hug. "We'll find her," she promised. Hope sprang into Louisa Nicholson's big brown eyes. Hope, and belief. Julie could have kicked herself. She'd had no right to make such a promise. Things could go wrong. Things did go wrong. Petty was convinced that the kidnapper was the same one who had taken the two young women. And one of them had been okay...

And one was still missing.

She'd had no right! No right to give that woman so much hope for her child. A beautiful little child with red hair and hazel eyes and those few adorable little freckles over her nose.

"Miss Hatfield!"

It was McCoy. He was at the door, waiting for her.

She offered Louisa a rueful smile. "Now I know why the feud began!" she whispered softly. She was rewarded with another half smile before she and McCoy left.

McCoy waited until they started down the walk before muttering darkly, "I wish to hell the ground hadn't been trampled to mush! We could have learned if she really was grabbed—"

"She was. Right here," Julie said.

He stopped dead still, his hands on his hips, his head at an angle, his silver eyes seeming to blaze out his ridicule.

"Oh, really?"

"Yes," Julie said flatly. She walked to the spot where Julie had been. "She was playing with her ball. A small ball, with little stars on it, kind of like a circus motif. Then it rolled out into the street and she came out. She looked both ways. She's really a very good little girl. It's a loving household. Of course, you don't have to be a psychic to have ascertained that."

McCoy shrugged and put on his sunglasses. "You'd be surprised," he said softly. "I've seen some awful things in some homes that looked like paradise on the outside."

Julie shook her head. "This is a good home, and Tracy loves it."

"If you say so."

Julie indicated the picture he was holding. "Look at her face!"

"All children have trusting faces," he said.

"That's not true, and you know it."

He was studying Tracy Nicholson's face. Julie leaned over his shoulder and looked at the smiling girl in the photograph. "Her hair is longer now," Julie said. "Oh, and she's had her braces off since this was taken."

"Has she?" McCoy opened the car door and gently tossed the picture inside. "Let's go."

"Wait, please."

"For what?"

"Just give me a minute, please? I want to show you what happened."

"Oh, come on—"

"Two minutes, Mr. McCoy."

He didn't dispute her again. He leaned against his car, watching her.

Julie started to follow Tracy's steps. "She caught her ball here. Then she saw the car come toward her and stop. The driver asked her to come closer. I think he said that he wanted directions. But Tracy was too smart. She wouldn't go to him. So he jumped out of the car and raced to her. He had something with him. A cloth. With some kind of dope on it. I don't know what. He came down this street with the intention of taking someone. He probably even watched Tracy before." She hesitated, then walked a bit. "This is where he took her from. He clamped the cloth over her mouth. And she fought until she lost consciousness."

She watched McCoy inhale and exhale. "Get in the car, Miss Hatfield. You can sit here and play charades. I have work to do."

"You are an arrogant buffoon! I only want to help you, and I can. And Petty says—"

"Yes, yes, Petty says. Okay, so Petty wants you in on this. And your friends inside want you in on this—"

"I've never met the Nicholsons before, McCoy, so they aren't my 'friends inside.'"

She couldn't see his eyes behind the sunglasses, but she could sense them narrowing. Speculatively. Maybe he was just beginning to believe...

"Get in the car, Miss Hatfield."

"Then—"

He stopped, glaring at her. "What kind of car, Miss Hatfield?"

"I don't know! I can't quite—"

"And is it a man driving? What does he look like? Is he alone? Is he tall, is he short?"

"I can't quite—"

"You're right. You can't. You can't give me a damn thing except that a little girl was kidnapped. Well, we all have that one figured out, Miss Hatfield."

"I've just told you—"

"Nothing! You haven't seen a thing."

"I've seen a lot! But no, I can't see everything, I'm not God! I've given you a good picture—"

"You've made some pretty good guesses. Now, let's go. I need to make phone calls. Set up a more organized search. I want to get out in the field myself. I—"

He broke off as the front door to the Nicholsons' house burst open, and Martin Nicholson was hurrying toward them.

"It came! A ransom call came. It wasn't long enough—they couldn't trace it. You've got to come in quickly. Petty is on the phone for you now."

McCoy could move faster than lightning. He was already on the phone with Petty by the time she came inside. Sunglasses pushed back on his head, he watched her as he grunted to Petty. Then finally he hung up the phone.

"The kidnapper has called. He wants a hundred thousand by tonight, small, unmarked bills, et cetera."

Julie nodded, feeling a tightening in her stomach. They had all suspected that this might be the same criminal.

Now they knew.

"You two seem to know something!" Louisa Nicholson said, fear rising in her voice.

McCoy exhaled softly. He shook his head. "Not really. Petty played the recording for me. Our man—or woman—is disguising his voice. But..."

"But what?" Julie said.

"Don't you know?" he taunted.

She stared at him, gritting her teeth. McCoy, to his credit, changed his tone quickly. Neither wanted the Nicholsons to realize that he didn't have faith in Julie.

"Our kidnapper seems to have eyes in the back of his head."

"He knows that the police are in on it already?" Julie asked softly.

"Oh, yes, he knows." McCoy watched her curiously. "He asked specifically for me to be the one to deliver the money."

"Where?" Julie asked.

He shrugged. "There's a phone booth by a gas station near the highway. I'll get the first call there."

Martin Nicholson stepped forward. "You will do it, Mr. McCoy, won't you?" he asked anxiously. "I'll get the money, I'll get it within an hour. There won't be any problem. I'll put the house up for what I don't have. The banks here will help out. They'll get the money for me by tonight. I don't want to take any chances."

"Mr. Nicholson—" McCoy began.

"It doesn't matter. The money doesn't matter at all. The house, none of it matters. Not without Tracy," he said.

Julie felt his pain so intensely, she could scarcely breathe.

"Mr. Nicholson," McCoy said quietly. "Of course, I'll take the money. Please, don't worry. The FBI likes to arrest kidnappers, too, especially the kind that travel over state lines. We don't like them to go on kidnapping other people. But please, I swear to you, we have a policy, and I have a personal commitment here, too. I swear that I'll not endanger your daughter's life in any way. Do you trust me?"

After a moment, Martin Nicholson nodded.

"Especially with Miss Hatfield along," Louisa Nicholson said.

McCoy looked at her, startled. "I should go alone. This might be dangerous—"

"Oh, Miss Hatfield!" Louisa's eyes were starting to fill with tears again. "You have to go along, please!"

"It isn't FBI policy—" McCoy began.

"On this case, it is," Julie reminded him pleasantly. Damn him, he still didn't quite seem to understand. The kidnapper could run them on a wild-goose chase. He could take the money, and fail to return Tracy Nicholson.

Maybe McCoy did understand. Maybe he just didn't believe she could do anything about it.

"I've got to get down to the bank right away," Mr. Nicholson said. "And get things in motion for the money."

There was a knock at the door. Tense, pale, Martin Nicholson threw open his front door. He seemed relieved. There were two uniformed officers there, a pretty young woman and a slender young man. "Is Lieutenant McCoy here?" the young man inquired.

McCoy nodded. "I'm here."

"I'm Jenkins, and this is Officer Daniels. She's going to stay with Mrs. Nicholson. I'll escort Mr. Nicholson to his bank and back here."

"Fine," McCoy said. "Mr. Nicholson, Mrs. Nicholson, I'll be back at seven. That will give us an hour before I'm supposed to be at the phone booth with the money. Miss Hatfield, if you're with me..." He waited, arching a brow at her.

Julie smiled reassuringly at the Nicholsons, then hurried along behind McCoy.

He had very long legs. He strode ahead of her to the car and got in. She thought he was going to gun the motor and escape without her.

But that wasn't his intention. She had nearly reached the car when he pushed open the passenger door from inside. "Get in, will you?"

She crawled into the car quickly. She was barely seated before they were pulling out onto the road.

"McCoy," she said, "I *am* coming with you tonight."

He didn't answer her.

"McCoy?"

"Damn it! Don't you know that these things can be dangerous? I've got to confer with Petty. We've got to be very careful. There's going to be backup on this, but it's damned hard when you're sent from phone booth to phone booth—and when this guy seems to have eyes in the back of his head. If you're with me, you could be putting your own life in jeopardy."

"How charming! I didn't realize that you were so concerned for my health and welfare."

His dark glasses were on but she could feel the heat of the glance he cast her way.

"Miss Hatfield—"

"The name seems to be giving you problems. Perhaps if you called me Julie—"

"Perhaps I would like it very much if I didn't have to speak to you at all!" he exploded.

"But you do have to speak to me! Damn you, don't you understand? I might be able to find Tracy. And that is the most important thing."

He was quiet for a long moment, then he sighed. "I do realize that Tracy is our priority. What do you think I am, Miss Hatfield, a block of ice?"

"Well—"

"Never mind, don't answer that. It's just that maybe I don't believe you can do Tracy any good."

"But what if I can?"

"I don't believe in—"

"You don't believe! But what if I *can* help Tracy? What if it's even a one out of a hundred shot? What if I could even make a lucky guess?" She had grown very passionate in her argument. She was almost touching him, she realized.

And then she felt a set of hot, electric fingers dancing a pattern down the length of her spine.

Julie moistened her lips. The passion remained in her voice. She had to convince him. "Give me the chance. Give Tracy the chance!"

"All right, all right, you're with me!" he exploded.

She settled back in her seat, strangely worn, as if she had just completed some great feat of manual labor.

"Where are we going now?" she asked.

"Back to see Petty first. I have to set up whatever cover I dare with him. There are the usual warnings. If I'm seen being followed, he'll kill the girl. We have to be very careful."

"Then where are we going?"

He cast her a quick look. "Dinner, Miss Hatfield. It's been a long day, and it's going to be a longer night. I haven't had a chance to eat. Any objections?"

Julie shook her head. "No," she said pleasantly. "No, none at all."

"If you really have any abilities, close your eyes and picture me the best steak in the area."

She sniffed and sat back. "I thought you knew where you were going around here."

"I do. But it's been awhile... well?"

"That's easy," Julie said softly. And she named her favorite steak house. "But how on earth you can eat—"

"Hunger. It does it every time," he told her. "Of course, I can leave you off—"

"And not come back for me," Julie said sweetly. "No, no, I think I can manage one meal with a McCoy."

But that same curious warmth that had traveled her spine seemed to have spread.

Was she going to share much more than one meal with this man?

For a moment, she saw darkness and shadows. And the silhouette of a man, a lover, walking slowly, surely toward her through those shadows...

The moon rose. She saw a scar etched across the man's shoulder.

And she felt the danger...

She shivered fiercely. All pictures faded away.

"Miss Hatfield?"

His voice was deep, sensual.

"I'm fine, Mr. McCoy. I was just wondering..."

"What?"

"Do you have a scar on your shoulder?"

He was very still. She wondered at first if he had heard her.

"Well, Miss Hatfield, if you ever see my shoulder bare, you'll get to find out, won't you?" he said, turning his attention to the road.

And she was left to wonder.

Chapter 3

McCoy was, Julie decided later, the ultimate professional. She watched him speak with the officers who would be assigned to wait patiently at various points in the region. There was a tremendous network of communication going on, for in a period of less than ten minutes, it was possible to go from West Virginia to Maryland to Virginia to West Virginia, and back through all three again.

And they were surrounded by countryside where a man could easily get lost among the foliage. Forests carpeted the mountainsides. In the darkness, movement could be tricky business. In certain areas, rock was sheer, with precipices that led nowhere—except straight down to more rock.

McCoy made it clear to the force working that night that they were in a difficult—perhaps in a no-win—

situation. The girl's life was most important, and they must do nothing to jeopardize little Tracy.

Sitting in the back while McCoy spoke to Petty, who would be manning phones and radio, and the six officers who would be assigned the task of trying very hard to be in the right place at the right time, Julie was startled by McCoy's knowledge of the region.

"How does he know this place so well?" she whispered to Pettigrew.

He grinned. "He grew up here, just the same as you did. Except he comes from a Maryland mountain and you come from a West Virginia mountain."

Julie frowned. Putting all the mountains together, they still hailed from a small region.

"Why haven't I ever seen him before?"

He took so long to answer, she wondered if Petty heard her. "Well, he's been gone for a long time, that's why."

"Then—"

"Any more, Miss Hatfield, and you'll have to look into that crystal ball of yours."

Julie sighed. He just didn't want to tell her any more about McCoy. Well, that was all right. All she had to do was get through the night with the man. Then she'd never have to see him again.

No. She would see him again. She knew it.

It was a quarter to six when they finished at the station and headed to the restaurant.

"Since you're from this area, why didn't you pick your own restaurant?" she asked him in the car.

"Because restaurants change constantly," he told her. "And it's been a long time since I've been home.

Is this it?" He pointed to the sign advertising the best steaks anywhere in the state.

"Yes."

"Is the advertising true?"

"I doubt it, but the food is good."

He smiled, pulled off the street and parked. To Julie's surprise, he walked to the passenger side and opened the door for her.

The beast came with manners on occasion, she thought.

Julie greeted the hostess who seated them, then smiled to the cute, young brunette, Holly, who waited on them.

The restaurant was brightly lit for a dinner place, with booths surrounding the walls, and tables covered with snow-white linen cloths. Julie was glad to be sitting across the table from McCoy at a well-lit booth rather than in a more romantic, candle-brimming room.

She needed distance with McCoy.

Holly, it seemed, didn't.

Even after McCoy ordered his steak and Julie ordered her salad, the young woman hovered until Julie formally introduced her to McCoy. Julie felt annoyed at the way Holly looked at McCoy, as if she had walked in with Mel Gibson or his equivalent.

"Are you staying in the area, Mr. McCoy?" Holly asked.

"Maybe, I'm not sure yet."

"Well, we certainly hope that you do. Don't we, Julie?"

"Oh, sure, yes, of course," Julie said blithely. McCoy cracked a crooked smile, which probably caused

Holly's heart to flutter. Finally, another couple came into the restaurant, and Julie and McCoy were left to sip their coffee in peace.

"A salad, huh?" McCoy said, pressing his fingertips to his temple. "Let me see. A vegetarian?"

"No," she said, trying to keep an edge out of her voice. "Just a very nervous person who is too worried about a little girl to dream of digesting a steak."

McCoy's hands moved idly over the heavy white coffee mug before him. They were large hands, with very long fingers. Well-kept hands. The fingertips were calloused, but the nails were neat and clean and bluntly clipped. To Julie's distress, she found herself imagining those hands against her skin. Covering her fingers. Moving softly against her arm.

She looked quickly into his eyes as he said, "I'm worried, too."

Julie would have responded, but Holly was back. She set a nice-size Caesar salad in front of Julie and a sizzling steak platter in front of McCoy.

Then the young woman proceeded to fuss. Did he want steak sauce? Sour cream for his potato?

"Butter for his beans?" Julie suggested pleasantly.

"Pardon?" Holly said, wide-eyed and innocent. "Oh." She blushed. "Oh, I know! More coffee."

She brought the pot. She filled McCoy's cup and forgot all about Julie's.

"Holly!"

"Oh, sorry," she said as she filled Julie's cup.

McCoy studied Julie when Holly left. "So the little blond angel has claws," he said softly.

"That's right," Julie agreed pleasantly. "And best you remember it."

"Should I?"

She arched a brow.

"Well, are we going to be together again for any reason in the future?"

"I don't know," Julie said evenly. "Are we?"

"You're the psychic."

"But you don't believe in me."

"All right. Let me ask you this. Is Tracy going to be all right?"

Julie looked at him across the table. "I don't know."

"Then . . ."

"I told you before. I'm not God. I can't see everything."

"Then what good is any of it?" he demanded, his tone suddenly so harsh that her fingers curled tightly around her cup. Instinct warned her that she should jump up and run.

"Sometimes, Mr. McCoy," she said quietly, meeting his hot silver gaze, "sometimes my ability can do an awful lot of good. Sometimes I can see people, I can see them exactly as they were . . . or are. Not every time, but sometimes. I don't know why I have this gift. When I am able to do something, I don't question it. I'm thankful for whatever the ability is. That's it. There's no more to it. I try. I try with all my heart. And on occasion, I have been able to save a life. And to me, Mr. McCoy, just one life is worth it all!"

She expected some burst of emotion from him in return. She didn't get it. He stared at her for what seemed the longest time, then he set his fork and knife into his steak again. His eyes were on his meal. "Just one life," he murmured.

"Pardon?"

"Nothing. Aren't you going to eat your salad?"

"For your information, Mr. McCoy—" Julie began, leaning close to him across the table.

"For my information what?" he snapped. His eyes blazed into hers. Little silver arrows seemed to pierce her flesh, to sweep inside her, raking through her with heat and fury. She didn't think she'd ever felt a look so physically before—ever.

Nor had she expected the anger that filled her, or that other emotion.

Attraction. Stark, sharp, physical attraction. So strong that it sizzled and whiplashed, and seemed to create electricity in the air between them.

She sat back. His gaze, too, was quickly masked, but Julie knew, suddenly and fiercely, that he had felt it.

"I..." She began. What? Her mind was a blank. She didn't even like him, she reminded herself dismally. And it didn't matter. They were out to catch a kidnapper. Possibly a murderer.

Tracy. They were out to save Tracy.

"What?" he demanded, exasperated.

"It's getting late," she said.

He glanced at his watch. It wasn't really so late, but he didn't dispute her.

"I'll get the check from your friend."

"I think she's *your* friend," Julie told him sweetly.

"Claws out, Miss Hatfield?"

"Hey, what do you want? I'm with a McCoy."

Two hours later they sat on the steps of a long walkway that led to an abandoned antebellum home outside the city limits of Harpers Ferry and Bolivar, but still on West Virginian soil.

Something felt right about being with him. Maybe it was his size. He was tall, with such impressive shoulders.

No...it didn't have anything to do with his size. He simply had that air of confidence about him.

Aggression, she warned herself. Bald aggression.

And no matter how strongly attracted she was, he was the last man she wanted to find herself involved with. She did not like being laughed at. Or doubted.

It was a beautiful spring night. Even in the shadows and darkness, shades of spring seemed to cover the land. The forests rose like deep, rich green sentinels, the sky was cast in cobalt and black, and the silver-white glow of the moon touched down on it all. Even where they were right now, with the night hiding the chipping paint of the old home, and the moonlight giving a past glory to the tall white columns on its porch, even the house looked beautiful.

But despite the warm spring air, Julie shivered. He was out there. With Tracy.

She closed her eyes. The phone should be ringing soon.

She gasped suddenly. Tracy.

She could see the little girl. And see what Tracy was seeing...

Darkness. Tracy was crying. It was hard to breathe. And hard to move, because she was boxed in. The smell around her was a rich one. Dirt.

"Oh, God!" she breathed.

"What, what?" McCoy demanded. His arm was around her shoulders. Tightly. Supportingly. Maybe he didn't believe—

Maybe he just felt the loneliness and the fear of the night.

She had to draw in a very deep breath. "He—he's got her buried," she said.

And just then, the phone rang.

McCoy leaped up, leaving the briefcase containing the money Martin Nicholson had obtained by Julie's feet. "Where?" he snapped into the receiver. McCoy was wired, so that the others would know where they were going next. He repeated the instructions given to him by the kidnapper.

When he hung up, Julie was already on her feet. "He hasn't left her enough air!" she said anxiously. "Where does he want us to go now?"

"Maryland side of the border," he said briefly. "Let's go."

Both of them were deadly silent as they moved on to the next phone booth. They barely reached it before the phone started ringing.

This time, McCoy came back to Julie looking perplexed. "He knows that I'm wired. And he knows exactly how many other cars are out."

"We have to do whatever he says!" Julie whispered softly. "She's running out of air. Tracy is running out of air."

He hesitated, gritting his teeth. Then he spoke loudly. "Petty, I'm getting rid of the wiring. He's on to us. And Julie says I don't dare take any more time."

Somewhere, Julie knew, Petty was cursing away. He didn't like the idea of putting her or Robert McCoy at risk.

But he liked the idea of what could happen to Tracy Nicholson even less.

"Come on," McCoy told Julie.

"Where now?"

"Virginia," he said curtly.

They drove to another phone booth, both hoping that the task force might still be around them. "How the hell does he know so damned much?" McCoy exploded. Then he mused softly. "Unless he's bluffing. Maybe he doesn't know. Maybe he's just guessing, and making darned good guesses."

"He's not bluffing about Tracy," Julie said.

They came to the next phone booth. The kidnapper had planned well. The phone booth was off the beaten track, away from any convenience stores or gas stations.

No one could have easily followed them to it.

And once again, just as McCoy stopped the car, it was ringing.

When he hung up that time, he came back to the car for the briefcase. "I'm walking it up the mountain," he told her.

"I'm coming with you."

"You're staying here—"

"Oh, no, I'm not! Don't you ever watch movies? The man always thinks he's being the hero by walking off alone into the night. And while he's gone, the monster comes back and gets the woman. I am not staying here alone."

He smiled. It was that same crooked smile that had so captivated Holly.

"You think there are monsters in these here hills, Miss Hatfield?"

"Yes, and more than just McCoys!" she answered sweetly. "Please! We're almost out of time."

He didn't argue with her any longer, but keeping up with him proved to be a trial for Julie.

She was mountain born and bred, and she could scamper up heights and over rocks with a fair amount of agility and ease.

But he had such long, long legs.

And it was apparent that he was mountain born and bred, too. He climbed without his breathing even deepening, and he seemed to have the agility of a mountain goat. He only turned back once or twice, however, reaching to drag Julie along with him.

Then they came to a plateau with a sparse clearing. "This is it," McCoy said.

"It's what?"

"It's where I'm supposed to leave the case."

Julie nodded. McCoy set the case down.

"Now what?" Julie asked.

He swore softly. "Now we go back to the phone."

"No!" Julie exclaimed suddenly.

"No? What do you mean, no?"

She shook her head fervently. "Tracy isn't here. She's—" Julie paused. "She's near the river. She can't hear the water rushing now because he's buried her. She couldn't even hear it once he had dragged her up. But she could see it. She could see it from the rock. And he thought it was funny. Really funny when he buried her. He kept laughing. He was careful, he didn't talk. But he laughed. There was something funny about it. Something really funny. He was so proud of himself. For being so bold. And he has no intention of letting her out."

"Where is she?" McCoy demanded harshly. He dropped the briefcase at his feet and grabbed Julie's shoulders. Roughly, he swung her around, studying her intensely. "Damn you, where is she? And if you're wrong, Julie Hatfield, I'll wring you out and hang you up to dry myself!"

"I'm not wrong!" she gasped. "I'm not wrong!" Julie shook her head. "She's not here, not here, not here..."

She paused, feeling the sensations as they began to steal over her. Tracy...

Tracy, where are you?

It came to her, slowly, then more quickly. Then frantically.

Can't breathe, can't breathe, can't breathe...

What happened, where are you?

Can't breathe, can't breathe, Mommy, where are you, please, I'm so scared...

Tracy...

And then Julie was with Tracy. She was with her as it had happened.

He was there. The kidnapper. And she was Tracy.

She was over his shoulder. He was panting, and they were climbing. Higher and higher. There were people around. No one could see Tracy, though. She was packed up like painting equipment. Lots of people sketched or painted here. They stopped, they milled around. They chatted, they saw things. Saw the rock, saw the water. Saw...

Tracy couldn't see, though. There was canvas over her head. She was still so dopey. She knew she needed to cry out. She couldn't. She felt him climbing. She'd been here before. It was so obvious.

And it was getting dark. Nearly dark. The people were gone, there were no lights. It was perfect. Such a perfect place to bury someone. And he had planned it all out. The hole was there, the box was there...

"Damnation!" McCoy shouted suddenly.

Julie's eyes flew open. She had been talking out loud, she realized. Describing what she had seen—and what she hadn't seen.

"What?" she cried.

"Come on, hurry up, I know the place you're talking about."

He had the briefcase in his left hand, her fingers in his right. With her in tow, he began to plunge down the mountainside, running, balancing, running harder.

She stumbled. He paused to pick her up. He halfway carried her all the way to the car.

Then he was on his radio, calling Petty. Demanding that he get the cars to the cemetery, telling him to get people up there right away.

It took them at least ten minutes to drive into town and park the car among all the official cars already there.

Then there was the climb up the pathway to the old cemetery.

When they reached it, Petty already had search lights going. He saw them across the broken and angled tombstones as they arrived. "Robert, are you sure?"

McCoy said something. Julie stopped in her tracks. Yes, yes, this was it!

Tracy, where are you?

Can't...breathe. Mommy, want Mommy, can't...

She could hear it. Julie could hear the awful, ragged, desperate sound as Tracy Nicholson struggled for the last of her air.

Julie spun around. She could hear it...

"There, over there!" she cried.

McCoy was ahead of her. "There's dirt plowed up here!" he shouted. There was a man nearby with a shovel. Without a word McCoy snatched it up and began to dig. Julie was quickly by his side. "Hurry, oh, hurry."

Mommy, Mommy, Mommy...can't breathe...

"Please, dear God, hurry!" Julie cried frantically. A pick lay nearby. Men were running toward them, but she was so desperate. She grabbed the pick and slammed into the ground.

Someone else was there. She looked up. It was one of Petty's regular men. Joe Silver. He smiled at her. "Julie, I'm stronger. Hand it over."

She did.

Joe swung the pick while McCoy shoveled.

"Easy!" she cried suddenly to Joe. The shovel struck something hard. She was afraid that the pick might crash through wood and enter into delicate flesh.

"It's some kind of a coffin, I think," McCoy said.

"It's a cemetery! There's probably hundreds of coffins up here!" Petty roared.

But not like this coffin, Julie knew. Her chest hurt. She couldn't speak because she couldn't breathe.

Tracy Nicholson was in that coffin, in the square box deep down in the hole. This time, the kidnapper had employed a truly bizarre sense of the macabre. Had his victim died, there would be no need to move her. Had she never been found, hundreds of years from now she might have been dug up just like any other corpse in the graveyard.

"Julie—" Petty began.

"Hurry!" She felt as if her chest were caving in on her. She gasped, deeply, desperately, drawing in air. "It's Tracy. She only has minutes left. He never intended to return her. Never."

Maybe Robert McCoy didn't believe in her, but he answered the desperation in her voice. He was down in the hole, having discarded the thought of attempting to drag up the box. Heedless of the dirt, he slammed the spade against the latch on the side of the coffinlike wooden box. There was an awful, wrenching sound. His hands on the rim, he tore at it. Julie heard the groaning of wood, then the lid gave at last to the power in his arms. There was a splintering sound, and the lid popped open.

And there was Tracy Nicholson.

She was just as Julie had seen her, dressed in her jeans and her pretty white shirt and her navy sweater. Her red hair was all tangled and askew.

Her freckled face was pale. Her eyes were closed. Her lips were silent.

"Dear God—" McCoy breathed.

She couldn't be dead, Julie thought. No, she just couldn't be dead. She would know; she would feel the loss.

McCoy had the silent girl in his arms and quickly stretched out on the ground. His fingers closed her nostrils as his lips descended over the girl's mouth, forcing air into her lungs.

Once, twice, three times...

Suddenly the little girl gasped, choked, coughed and choked again. Her little chest rose and fell on its own. "Oh, thank God!" Julie shrieked. McCoy moved aside. Tracy's eyes were opening. She looked right at Julie.

"Thanks," she mouthed softly.

Her eyes closed again, but she was still breathing. Evenly.

A cheer went up in the cemetery. Almost loud enough to wake the dead, Julie thought. And that was almost what they had done. A few more minutes, and there wouldn't have been a prayer for Tracy. Julie was shaking. She had seen. Yes, she had seen Tracy. But she hadn't seen the cemetery. She would have never made it on her own.

McCoy...

He had known what she was saying. He hadn't believed, but he had taken a chance.

He was looking at her now. She was on her knees in the middle of all the dirt that he had dug up. She was covered in it.

So was he.

"Make way for the medics!" someone called.

"Her parents are here, down on the street," someone else said.

"Here's the doctor!"

"And her folks!"

The Nicholsons didn't notice either McCoy or Julie as they rushed for Tracy. "My baby!" Louisa shrieked. Tracy's eyes opened at the sound of her mother's voice. She didn't seem to have any strength, but she could talk.

"Mommy! I called you. I called you and called you."

"And I'm here, my dearest, I'm here, I'm here."

Tracy was quickly wrapped in her mother's arms. Martin Nicholson supported his wife as she stood with their child. The two of them turned away, stunned with the wonder of their daughter's return.

People were following behind them, Petty and Joe Silver and some of the other officers. The hole in the earth still lay gaping open. There would be investigative work on it. Fingerprints would be taken, the area would be searched for the minute clues.

But for the moment, it was just a hole. This time, the grave had been cheated.

They were nearly alone. And McCoy was still staring at Julie. Then suddenly his arms were on her and he was lifting her, nearly throwing her into the air.

"Damn it, we did it! We made this one, we made it!"

And as he dropped her, she came sliding down against his chest. She felt the tight, hot ripple of muscle in his arms, in his torso. She felt the silver fever of his eyes, blazing into hers.

Then she felt the rough, searing enthusiasm of his kiss as his lips suddenly and passionately covered hers.

Lightning seemed to strike. Julie might have heard thunder crashing across the heavens.

Heat, startling, sweet, astounding, swept in her and throughout her.

He started to raise his lips, started to pull away.

But he did not...

His mouth settled more firmly on hers, and his arms wound around her. A searing pressure forced her lips to part for his. The amazing fever held her still in his grip, responding almost savagely to his touch, tasting his mouth, savoring the feel...

Oh, no! This just couldn't be right. She wanted to go on and on.

She barely knew him.

No, she had met him in a dream.

Demon or lover?

She didn't know. All she did know was that the electricity was nearly more than she could bear, that she had never felt like this about any man, anywhere, be it real or in a dream. And it was wrong. He didn't even believe in her...

But she didn't pull away. He was the one to do so, his arms still around her, his eyes a silver fire as they stared into hers.

"Now this—is madness!" he said hoarsely.

Julie pulled furiously away from him. They were alone with an open grave site and dozens of broken-down tombstones. Voices were growing faint in the distance.

"Yes, it is. You don't even like me, do you?" Julie accused him.

"I never said that—"

"Well, it is certainly extreme madness," Julie insisted. "The moon is out, that's my only excuse. Really. A handshake would have sufficed!" Confused, flushed, dismayed, she turned, nearly stumbling over one of the old tombstones. He caught her arm. She wrenched it free. "Good night, Mr. McCoy." Determined not to trip again, Julie kept walking. She heard his soft laughter behind her.

"Miss Hatfield?"

"What?"

"Am I going to see you again?"

"No!"

Again, his laughter touched her. She spun in a new fury. "All right, McCoy, what is it now?"

"All right, Miss Hatfield. You're the psychic. But you're wrong. I will see you again. I'm very certain of it."

And smiling like a self-satisfied cat, he shoved his hands into the pockets of his black leather jacket and sauntered confidently past her.

Chapter 4

McCoy was right.

Julie did see him again, and much sooner than—but certainly not where—she had expected.

Just five days later she saw him in church, sitting just a few rows ahead of her. He was with a tall, slim woman with dark sandy hair and two children. An uneasiness spread throughout her. She hadn't thought that he could be married.

No, she couldn't be his wife. Not even someone with McCoy's inborn arrogance could have kissed her the way he did if he had a wife.

Still...

When the woman turned enough so that Julie could see her face, she saw that the woman was beautiful. She had bright blue eyes and fine, stunning features. At her side was a little girl, maybe a year or two older than Tracy Nicholson. She had soft, pale blond hair that waved down her back. She must have sensed Julie watching her, because she turned and her eyes met Julie's. She smiled. It was a wonderful smile.

Then the boy turned, too. He was about twelve. His eyes weren't blue. They were that steel gray color, just like McCoy's.

So he did have a wife and family...

No, he couldn't have. She was certain she would have known.

Maybe not. Inner sight could be blind at the strangest times.

The woman, realizing that the two children were staring at someone or something behind them, turned, too. Of course, she caught Julie staring right at her.

She smiled.

Well, it was time.

McCoy turned, too.

He wasn't in his black jacket, but neither had he really dressed for church. No one really dressed up in the spring and early summer; they didn't want the many tourists in the area to feel awkward for dressing casually. Julie was casual herself in a short denim skirt and short-sleeved tailored white blouse. A little bit of warmth went a long way. She was wearing sandals and no stockings.

McCoy wore black trousers and a turquoise knit shirt. The buttons were open at his neck. She didn't meet his eyes. She was staring at the tiny space of chest covered with coarse, sandy whorls of hair that was just visible at the opening of his shirt. He was tanned, so the skin beneath the springy feel of hair would be bronze. And tight. He was very well muscled. A powerful man. She had noted that when he had ripped the coffin open, and she had felt it the several times that he had touched her.

Her eyes met his. She was suddenly convinced that Robert McCoy had a few powers of his own. He'd been reading her mind. And of course, her mind had been on his body.

Right in the middle of the last amen!

He smiled. Smiled just as he had the night they had found Tracy. Smiled like a man who knew something. As if he held something over her.

She nodded briefly, then tore her eyes from his and looked straight ahead.

But by then, the service was ending. And when she slipped from her pew and started out, she stiffened. She didn't need to turn to realize that he was right behind her.

As soon as they stepped from the church and into the daylight, she felt his hand on her arm, stopping her. "Why, Miss Hatfield! Good morning. Were you in there praying for divine guidance?"

She spun, smiling sweetly. "On the contrary, Mr. McCoy. No one wants to see things that others don't."

He arched a doubting brow, then turned quickly as the woman he had been with emerged from the church. "Julie Hatfield, this is my sister, Brenda Maitland. Of course, underneath she's really a McCoy. Being as you're a Hatfield, I feel obliged to remind you of such a thing."

"Oh, Miss Hatfield!" Brenda Maitland extended a hand to her and offered her a broad smile. "How nice to meet you. And how very wonderful that the two of you found that little girl." She shivered, looking up the cliff toward the old cemetery. The church was on the pathway that led to the burial ground. The view from the church was stunning. There was the street, which was part of the National Park Service now, handsome with its ages-old buildings. And there were the rivers, the Shenandoah meeting the Potomac, beautiful blue with little whitecaps as water rushed over rapids. Then there were the mountains stretching onward, the spring greenery of Maryland Heights.

To reach the church from the valley below was easy enough. Some of the original settlers had carved steps right out of the rock. The climb became more difficult once there were no more steps, but the mountain residents were accustomed to climbs. It was the tourists who panted as they walked the trek to Jefferson rock and onward to the cemetery.

But all in all, it was a long climb to reach that cemetery.

"We're so close to where it all happened. Imagine! Someone managed to bring that box up there, dig a big hole, then drag that poor little girl up, and no one even noticed all of it going on!"

It was extraordinary, Julie thought. Especially when they were already into the spring tourist season.

"But it turned out well, at least," Julie said.

"Are you really a witch?"

Julie started at the softly spoken question that seemed to come from nowhere. She looked down. The little girl with her mother's blue eyes and the beautiful cascade of blond hair was standing right before her.

"A witch?" Julie repeated.

"Well, Uncle Robert said that—"

"Tammy!" Brenda said, distraught.

"Did I say witch?" McCoy asked, his hands on his niece's shoulders, his eyes sizzling as they touched Julie's with no apology whatsoever.

Fine. Julie looked from McCoy to his niece. "I don't cook with toads or snake's eyes or anything like that, if that's what you mean. I'm sorry."

"But you are a witch in a way, right?" Tammy insisted.

"Well, I think your uncle is convinced that I am," Julie said sweetly.

"Let me finish the introductions," McCoy interrupted. Still no apology, but he was suddenly determined not to let it go any further. "This impudent little piece of baggage is Tammy Maitland. And my nephew here is Taylor Maitland. We were on our way to Sunday brunch. Care to join us?"

"Oh, no, I—" Julie began.

"Oh, please!" Tammy insisted.

"I really—"

"Please? I promise, I won't ask you anything more about being a witch!"

Julie gazed at the little girl. What if I told you that your uncle really doesn't like me? That I spent the majority of a night with him and he still didn't believe in a single thing I told him?

"Please, do come," Brenda insisted. "Of course, I suppose that you have been hounded. Robert was saying that you were lucky you're not an official, and that you could crawl away to that house of yours up in the mountain. The station was just plagued with phone calls from newspapers and the television stations. Fending off the media is worse than coping with the criminals at times, so my brother tells me. We really won't plague you. Yes, we will, but just a little."

Julie had to laugh. She was surprised then to catch McCoy's silver gaze upon her. And she was startled by the softness of his voice when he bid her a simple, "Come?"

Julie shrugged. "I suppose. Artemis will miss my speedy return."

"Who's Artemis?" Taylor asked.

Julie widened her eyes. "Artemis? He's my cat. My black cat," she added, smiling as she looked at McCoy. "My familiar, I believe."

He groaned. "Shall we go?"

They went. Julie didn't need to speak with McCoy as they walked to their cars because Brenda Maitland managed to keep Julie at her side. "You'll have to forgive my brother. His feelings on this subject are wickedly single-minded. Of course, it is natural, I suppose." She seemed grave. "After everything that happened."

Julie's curiosity was instantly piqued. "What happened?" she asked.

But her question came too late. Brenda didn't hear it. She had stopped to look back. "Where's Taylor now?"

"Up here with me," McCoy called. They had reached the church's small parking lot. "Miss Hatfield, will you ride with us?"

"I have my own car," Julie said.

"I'll get you back to it."

She hesitated. He hadn't gotten her back to her car the last time she had seen him. Of course, that hadn't really been his fault. She'd been so mad that she'd stayed with Petty until he'd been able to drive her to her car.

"But I—"

"Come on!" He walked to her. His body blocked her from the others. "You're dangerous on the road, you know."

"I am not."

"You should have seen me coming."

"You should have seen *me* coming."

"No, Miss Psychic. You should have *seen* me coming!"

"Oh, no, I'm not going through this—"

"Yes, you are. Come on." He raised his voice. "She's driving with us."

"Great!" Brenda called, climbing into the back of her brother's Lincoln along with the children.

"I never said—"

"What's the matter, don't you like kids?"

"I like kids just fine. I have problems with adults at times!"

"I won't spill a thing or throw a single pea, I promise," McCoy vowed gravely.

He was shoving her again. Or dragging her. One or the other. She was nearly in the passenger seat and she hadn't agreed in the least.

But she couldn't disagree, because McCoy was quickly in the driver's seat, and they were already moving. And while they drove, Julie discovered that she hadn't seen Brenda before because McCoy's sister usually attended a little church two towns over.

"Why were you in today?" Julie asked.

"Oh, Robert convinced me. Quite honestly? I wanted to meet you. And Robert said that you'd be there today."

Julie cast McCoy a quick glance. Petty knew she came to church here almost every Sunday. He could have told McCoy.

But had he?

Julie wondered again at Brenda's comments about her brother—that it was natural for him to feel the way he did about psychics. Why?

The question plagued her, but she couldn't ask it now. Yet as she studied McCoy, she felt a trembling steal over her fingers again. Was he the man in her dream? Her cheeks felt hot as she remembered the dream. It had been so real. She could almost feel the man's body. They had been so close, so intimate. She barely knew McCoy.

His eyes touched hers suddenly. Silver. Sharp. Like blades, they seemed to pierce right through her.

He knew, she thought in a sudden panic. He knew what was going on in her mind!

He couldn't. She tore her eyes from his. He looked at the road. He was smiling.

He hated psychics, he wanted to deny them all. But the way he had just looked at her...

A hot sizzle streaked along her spine. He could deny it, but Julie was absolutely convinced that Robert McCoy had certain powers of his own.

And oh, the things that he could read in her mind!

"Have you always lived here, Miss Hatfield?" Taylor asked.

"Always," she said softly.

"A Hatfield from the hills!" Brenda said, laughing softly.

"Well, it seems to me that these hills are brimming with McCoys," Julie returned good-naturedly.

"Yes, I suppose it's true. We have lots of cousins around us. Of course you're the first Hatfield I've ever met," Brenda said. "Do you think there really was a feud at one time?"

"Think?" McCoy snorted. "I could almost guarantee it—seeing as how we've met a Hatfield now."

"Whoa!" Brenda protested. "Julie, ignore him!"

"Oh, don't worry about it," Julie said. "I have it on the highest authority that there was a feud—and that the Hatfields won. So there."

Brenda laughed softly. Julie felt a silver gaze on her, and she quickly looked down.

Her fingers were trembling again. She could feel the man's warmth as if it touched her.

What is he doing to me? she wondered.

They were barely friends. They were more likely enemies.

She had never wanted anyone more. She felt the tension building in the car between them. Bit by bit. The air didn't seem to touch her. The heat was building. Explosively.

Brenda was talking. About something. Julie couldn't hear her. She suddenly wanted to be alone with McCoy. She wanted to shout at him. She wanted to tell him to leave her alone, to get out of her life.

And if he didn't...

Well, then, he needed to hold her.

No. He needed to make love to her.

The car pulled off the road. They had reached the restaurant in Charlestown.

Julie nearly catapulted from the car. Taylor was emerging behind her, pointing out a place where his Little League team had played the year before, and thankfully, a feeling of normalcy settled over her once again.

She didn't know about McCoy. He had already walked into the restaurant.

Once they were all inside and seated and Julie had a cup of steaming black coffee in front of her, she felt better. The brunch buffet featured all sorts of magnificent things to eat, and when Julie returned with her plate, she was surprised to see that McCoy's choice of foods might have been a copy of her own. They had both piled their plates high with peel-and-eat shrimp and marinated artichokes and sweet-and-sour pickles.

"I'm going back for an omelet and red meat later," McCoy assured her, pulling back her chair. And at that moment, she had to smile.

The meal progressed. Brenda Maitland's children were charming and very well behaved. There was a closeness to their family group that she found herself enjoying.

Maybe the Hatfields had won the feud, but it hadn't done much for her. She was an only child, and her mom had passed away over ten years ago, her dad a year ago last spring. She did have aunts and uncles and cousins, but they had slowly moved toward the big city, Washington, D.C. She saw them as often as she could.

But then, McCoy lived in Washington, she remembered. And he would probably be going back there. Soon.

"Tell us more about Tracy Nicholson," Brenda said suddenly. "She really wasn't much help to the police after she was found, was she?"

Julie shrugged and glanced at Robert. "Your brother knows more about that than I do. I wasn't there when they questioned her. Tracy had been taken to the hospital immediately, and they questioned her there. I wasn't needed anymore, and there were plenty of people who were."

"She didn't see anything," Robert said. "Nothing at all. She couldn't even tell us what kind of car it was."

"I know," Julie murmured.

"You know?" McCoy said.

Julie gritted her teeth to hang on to her temper. "When we were at the house, when I was coming down the steps, I saw the ball go into the road. Then I saw the car. But it was—it was in a mist."

"How convenient," McCoy said dryly.

Brenda elbowed her brother. "Did you see the man, Julie? *Was* it a man?"

Julie shook her head. "Yes, I think so. I mean, I think it's a man. But no, I didn't see him. He must have been..." She paused, her voice breaking off. She had a sensation of...

"A stocking!" she exclaimed suddenly.

"What?" McCoy demanded.

"That was it!" She stared at him. "He scared Tracy right from the start because his face was so strange. He had a stocking pulled over his face. He wanted to make sure that she didn't see him!"

"But she would have run right away," Brenda protested.

"No, no," Julie said excitedly. "She was already in the road, remember? She was smart, but she was scared. And he realized just how smart she was quickly, so he jumped out of the car to take her."

"But what a dangerous thing to do!" Brenda exclaimed. "For the kidnapper, I mean. Anyone could have seen him. And he wouldn't have looked normal in the least. How recklessly brazen—"

"Brazen and smart, and laughing at the pack of us all the while," McCoy muttered. "Brenda, somehow this guy walked to the cemetery, dug a hole, planted a box and then a little girl. I have no problem seeing him as brazen or reckless."

"Well, Julie has just explained to you why Tracy Nicholson can't help you."

"Why can't she tell me about the car?" he demanded. He stared straight at Julie.

"Tracy doesn't know cars," Julie said softly. "And there—there was mist around it."

McCoy sat back. His gaze was an open challenge. "What mist? There was no fog that day. Nothing. Unless a little cloud descended right around the kidnapper's car."

"No, of course not—"

"Then why can't you tell me about the car?"

Julie sighed. "I can only tell you what Tracy saw. My connection always seems to be with the victim."

"That's convenient, too," McCoy commented dryly.

"Excuse him for being so rude," Brenda said with a long sigh. "He can be such a pest."

"I've noticed."

"Maybe he knows that," Taylor said suddenly.

They all started. The children had been so quiet that Julie had forgotten Taylor and Tammy had been listening. Now they stared at the handsome boy with McCoy's steel-gray eyes.

"What was that, Taylor?" Brenda said to her son.

"I'm talking about the kidnapper. He must know something about the people around here, right? He wanted Uncle Robert to carry the case. And maybe he knew something about Julie." He stared at his uncle. "He meant to kill the little girl he kidnapped, right? He meant to kill her all along. So why cover his face to Tracy? Unless he knew that Julie was going to be called in, and that she might be seeing him through the little girl's eyes?"

They were all dead silent for the longest time, staring at Taylor in amazement.

His words had made so much sense.

"Well, I'll be darned," McCoy said softly. "That's great reasoning, Taylor."

Taylor flushed, pleased. McCoy tousled his hair. "Of course, it's possible, too, that the kidnapper knew that he was running the risk that Tracy might be found before she did run out of air."

"Maybe," Julie murmured. Then she suddenly gazed at Brenda, feeling guilty. "And maybe we shouldn't be talking about this all in front of your children—"

"Are you kidding?" Brenda demanded. "I want them to know what happened, *and* what almost happened. That way, they'll watch out for one another, and they'll be doubly careful. It's not the same world we grew up in, Julie. Children have to be aware of the maniacs out there. They have to be. For their own safety."

"We're very careful, Mom. Aren't we, Taylor?" Tammy demanded.

Taylor nodded. "I'm right about the kidnapper, though. I know it. He's not afraid of his victims seeing him. He's afraid of Julie seeing him."

A chill streaked along Julie's spine. Was Taylor right?

McCoy groaned. "Not another psychic, please. This is all getting unbearable."

"You know your uncle doesn't believe in psychics," Brenda reminded her son gently.

"You don't believe in Julie?" Tammy asked.

"Not a whit," McCoy replied pleasantly. "Where is the waitress? We could use more coffee."

"And we could use more milk," Tammy agreed. "But if you don't believe in Julie, why did you make her come to breakfast?"

Brenda gasped. Julie felt a grin tugging at her lips, then she felt McCoy's eyes on her again.

"Well, she is attractive, isn't she?"

"Beautiful," Taylor agreed, and then blushed. Julie felt her cheeks growing red. McCoy could be so light and personable one minute, and then come down like lead the next. She could almost like the man, and then . . .

"The most beautiful charlatan I've ever come across," he said smoothly.

"Maybe I can entice the waitress to serve the coffee over his head," Brenda murmured. "Robert—"

Julie had had enough. She was suddenly heedless of Brenda and heedless of the children. She leaned closer to McCoy. "If I'm such a charlatan, how did we find that little girl?" she demanded.

"Luck, maybe," he replied, his gaze hard. "Perhaps you even noticed him going through town. Maybe you saw someone with a spade heading for the cemetery."

"I don't even live in town!"

"Maybe a friend mentioned it."

"But I didn't know it was a cemetery. You're the one who found the cemetery, McCoy!"

"Look, I'm not trying to say that you lie on purpose—Hatfield. But perhaps you build on some sort of suggestion in your mind—"

"I was with that child, and you know it!"

"Well, her parents think so, and that's enough, isn't it? Petty is fooled." He looked quickly at Brenda. "Joe Silver and I were the ones digging away, covered in dirt, and the Nicholsons just wanted to thank Julie. It's a great life, right?"

"Don't you believe in anything?" Julie exclaimed.

"Oops, here's the waitress!" Brenda said cheerfully. "I think they both need a bath in cold water, but we'll take a little more coffee, please. And milk for the kids. And the check, if you don't mind," Brenda said.

She kept talking cheerfully, determined to keep up a monologue so Julie and McCoy would both shut up. And they did.

But through the rest of the meal, Julie could feel his eyes on her. And more.

She could feel the heat rising again. It was anger. Really. He was so arrogant, so damned sure of himself.

Was it really anger?

She had become tense. The brush of his napkin over her fingers nearly made her jump a mile. He glanced her way. She stared furiously at him. *Don't you dare call me a charlatan!* she silently yelled at him.

But you are, you have to be...

She gritted her teeth. She was not reading his mind—she didn't read minds. And she wasn't a witch. Still, she could scarcely sit in the restaurant a minute longer. She had to do something.

Touch him.

Her heart was pounding too quickly; she had difficulty breathing. And it seemed that a sizzle of fire danced up and down her spine.

Just when she didn't think she could take another minute, McCoy stood. "I'll just pay up front."

"I'll leave the tip," Julie said, leaping up. McCoy might have argued with her. Then she realized that he was in as big a hurry as she was.

But if Brenda was aware of their distress, she gave no sign. When they reached the car she nimbly climbed into the backseat saying, "Robert, drop the kids and me off first, will you? As long as you don't mind, Julie."

No! Julie wanted to shriek.

She kept her jaw locked. McCoy grunted some kind of an agreement.

As he started the car, he slid his dark glasses on against the bright glare of the spring day. Julie sat silently in her seat, noting the way the wind tousled his hair. She looked straight ahead. She wanted to strangle the man. She had also been tempted to reach out and run her fingers over the rugged line of his cheek.

He pulled off the highway to follow a small, winding pathway up to an old farmhouse. He stopped in front of it. "Well, this is home," Brenda said, getting out with the children. She paused to stand by Julie's window and shake her hand. "Can you come in?"

"Oh, thank you. But I think I'd best get home myself," Julie said.

Brenda nodded. "Well, we won't be strangers now. We live close by each other. And I'll even admit defeat in the feud for the McCoys, if we can all be friends now!"

Julie laughed. "I really haven't the faintest idea who won," she said. "And it was wonderful to meet you."

The kids told her goodbye and ran around to kiss their uncle goodbye. Then Julie and McCoy were back on the road. Neither of them spoke.

When they neared the lot where her car was parked, Julie spoke at last. Politely. "Thank you for brunch. Your sister is lovely."

"Thank you," he said curtly. He came to a stop. He was going to get out to open her door, but Julie moved too quickly.

"I'm fine, thank you. Goodbye, McCoy."

"Miss Hatfield—"

"Don't you mean, 'Miss Charlatan,' McCoy?" she asked, her door half open.

"You've known my opinion—"

"Well, then, I'll tell you mine. You, sir, are an ass!"

With that, she slammed his car door shut and hurried to her own vehicle. She smiled grimly—she could hear the thunder of his retort following her.

She ignored it, revved up and quickly swung from the parking lot.

Several minutes later, her smile faded.

He was following her.

Just how mad had she made him? she wondered. And despite herself, she felt a jumping in her heart.

She was almost home. And he was following her still. Right to her house.

Well, she'd wanted to have a fight with him. A real, live fight.

She wanted to vent some frustration. To hit him good.

She just didn't want him to hit back.

And that annoying sizzle of heat was back, racing up and down her spine...

She pulled off the highway, and up the long patch that led to her house. She parked in the big expanse of her front yard, slamming out of the driver's seat to await him.

He braked to a halt right behind her and got out.

"What!" Julie shrieked. "You have to follow me to hand out more abuse! You are an ass, a complete fool, as hardheaded as rock. And you had no right to follow me just to argue that point. You—"

"I followed you, Miss Hatfield, because you left your purse in my car!" he bellowed in return.

"Oh. Oh!"

For a moment Julie just stood there, a column of fury and tension. She strode quickly to where he leaned against his car door, holding her small white leather clutch bag. "Thank you!" she snapped, taking the bag and hurrying to her front door.

He was right behind her. She opened the door, and he followed her in.

"And I'm an ass, am I? You tell me, Miss Hatfield, what happens when this voodoo doesn't work? When you have people believing in you and following your every lead. Only you're leading them down the wrong damned path?"

"I don't go down the wrong path!"

"Well, just what happens if you do?" he demanded heatedly.

He was backing her down the hallway, past the stairs to the rear wall.

Then she was against the wall, and his hands were on her shoulders. His body was nearly touching hers; she could feel his fingers so acutely through the thin fabric of her blouse.

"I don't owe you any answers, McCoy!" she flared. "You're in my house—and I don't remember inviting you in!"

He stopped, suddenly seeming to realize that he'd barged in.

"I'm leaving!"

"Good! Fine!"

"And I won't be back, Miss Hatfield. We've done what we were supposed to do. It's over. I don't have to see you again."

"And I don't have to see you again. I don't have to listen to you, I don't have to talk to you!" Julie said.

"That's right," he agreed savagely. He was still touching her, though. His hands were still on her shoulders.

He dropped them. Julie gritted her teeth.

He turned, striding to the front door, which he opened and slammed shut behind him.

Julie winced at the sound. She leaned against the wall, closing her eyes. If only her heart would stop beating so stridently. If the pulse that throbbed against her temple would slow down.

If only the sudden . . .

Emptiness, yes, emptiness . . .

Would go away.

There was a thundering on her door. She started, then yanked it open.

He was back. McCoy was back. Tall, imposing, towering there in her doorway.

"What—what else did I leave in your car?" she demanded.

"Nothing," he said briefly.

"Then?"

He could be a bully when he wanted. He stepped inside, closing the door behind him.

Julie backed up just a bit, watching him.

He pulled off his sunglasses, and in his eyes she saw a tumult that matched her own. She swallowed, and her eyes lowered to his throat, and she saw the same pulse beating there.

"Then?" She repeated softly. "What . . ."

He groaned. "Then—then this!" he stated flatly. Suddenly he was reaching out, and she was drawn irrevocably into his arms. His mouth was on hers, wet, hot, open. Demanding. Parting her lips. And all the heat and electricity that had played between them suddenly met and seemed to explode there in the hallway like soaring red fireworks. The fever scorched along her back and settled into her.

And the kiss went on and on...

The kind of kiss that could never, never stop at the lips.

Chapter 5

His kiss was the most wonderful thing Julie had imagined, sweet water on dry earth, magic and mystery, and a slow, burning lesson in the ways of sensuality. His lips touched her lips, but the fire they created touched her skin, swirled to her belly and found root in some central place of her being. Every shift, every movement, each touch, each stroke...all were so natural and fluid, and all touched her anew. She felt the roughness of his fingertips against the bare flesh on her arms, her cheeks. His lips, his tongue...he kissed her and kissed her. Tasting, demanding. Savagely and tenderly at the same time. The feel of his body against hers was overwhelming. The driving tension, the engulfing heat, the steel power seemed to enwrap and encompass her. Then his lips rose briefly, and his eyes touched hers. She didn't know exactly what he sought, but he seemed to have found it. Once again, his lips found hers. His teeth gently caught her lower lip, and the searing warmth streaked through her once again. Her knees were weak, and a fierce trembling had begun within her.

His tongue bathed her lower lip, then he kissed her cheek, her forehead, her lips again. His movement was slow...

And so anxious. So leashed. As if he hungered greatly, but dined slowly to savor each morsel of a meal.

Julie gasped softly, clinging to his neck. He brushed aside her hair and kissed her throat. His tongue teased her flesh; his teeth barely brushed it. His lips moved again, just beneath her ear. Then lower, against her shoulder.

The buttons of her blouse were slipping open. As if they had life of their own, as if they approved of the assault on her senses, as if they gave blessing to it. He found the flaring throb of her pulse and left his kiss there. And then his head moved lower, and she vaguely thought that he had wonderful, thick rich sandy hair, then the thoughts were stolen from her mind, for his kiss was pressed against the rise of her breast, searing hot and more arousing than she could bear. She moaned softly, and her fingers knotted into his hair.

"Julie..."

"Yes..."

She didn't know if the whisper of her name was a question or not. She knew only that he had touched her in some way from the first moment she had seen him. And they had both known that coming to this point was inevitable.

He was the man . . . the man in her dream. The man who had brought heaven to her, here on this earth. The man who . . .

A chill swept through her. Danger. There had been so much danger in the dream. Ecstasy followed by fear.

But she wasn't afraid.

Perhaps he felt her tensing. Perhaps not. His arms were more securely around her. His kiss was more tantalizing. No fear . . .

Either that, or the desire was simply greater. So great that she could not care. Her blouse had fallen open all the way. He moved deftly, swiftly, knowing what he wanted. His fingers brushed against her back, freeing her breasts from the restraints of her white lace bra. His lips kissed the rise of flesh, then his mouth took her in, his tongue brushing her nipple fiercely, his hands . . . caressing.

A long, low moan escaped her. All thoughts of fear evaporated. She had never felt more sheltered.

Or more aroused.

His lips covered hers once again, then his head rose suddenly and she felt the silver fever of his eyes tense on hers. She was in his arms, half naked now, parts of her clothing barely dangling from her shoulders.

"You do live alone, I hope?" he said.

She smiled, a slow, warm smile that curled across the fullness of her lip. She nodded.

Then she was swept urgently into his arms. Her arms curled around his neck.

"Where?" he demanded huskily.

"Upstairs."

Julie closed her eyes and leaned against him, secure in his hold. McCoy took the stairs two at a time.

There were five doors on the second floor, all standing ajar.

Perhaps he did have a touch of some form of power within his own doubting heart, for he chose the second door, the one that led to her bedroom. It was a beautiful room, with age-old mahogany furniture and a bed with a tall canopy and a plush, deep red, patterned comforter that matched the valances above the lighter drapes. Julie was glad she had made her bed that morning.

And then she knew it would not have mattered in the least because McCoy managed to one-handedly strip off the comforter and top sheet before placing her within that cocoon of covers. He came with her, not just a graceful lover, but an urgent one, his lips finding hers again before her head touched the pillow. Graceful, able, nearly frantic. His kiss broke as he found her shoes and dropped them heedlessly to the floor, his eyes on hers. Julie simply watched him for a moment, then she roused herself, shimmying from the remnants of her top garments and reaching out for him. Her fingers seemed so small and delicate against his chest as she worked at the two buttons on the turquoise knit shirt. Perhaps she didn't move them quickly enough. A strangled sound seemed to escape him, and he wrenched the shirt over his shoulders. For a moment they paused on their knees, watching one another, and then he pulled her into his arms, and the feel of her naked breasts against his hair-roughened chest was exquisite.

His hands covered her as he pressed her to the bed again, then he found the zipper at the rear of her skirt, and the rasp as it went down seemed to fill Julie with an ever greater longing. He slipped the skirt from her hips and she was left in a wisp of white lace bikini underwear, and for the first time, something gave him pause.

He stared at her as seconds ticked by. Then he touched her lip, and delicately drew a line from her mouth along her throat, between her breasts, down past her naval and straight to the throbbing center of all her heat and desire. She moistened her lips, amazed that such a delicate touch could create such a sensation. She could lie there no longer, her body on fire. She started to rise, but he pressed her back, his lips covering hers, then tracing that same pattern he had already drawn down the length of her body with his finger.

Julie twisted violently as the sweet sensation tore wildly through her. A flick of his finger had broken the thin band on the panties, and the wisp of lace was tossed away with no apology. And once again, she found the heat and desire within her rising to an unbearable point, half agony and half ecstasy, the longing and the pleasure so acute.

Then he was with her. His own clothing was shed and strewn, and the magnificent warmth of his body covered all of her. She entwined her arms around his neck and touched his lower lip gently with the tip of her finger. She stroked his shoulders, her fingers trailing down his back. He groaned, and she brought her delicate, sweeping touch around, teasing his midriff, his hip. Lower. Closing her fingers around him...

Some harsh sound emitted from him and it was over, this brief, sweet time of play and exploration.

It could be no other way.

Julie wrapped her arms and legs around him, welcoming him as he thrust into her, gasping, shivering, trembling, as she accepted the whole of him. He paused. He moved so slowly. Drawing out the touch, the wonder...

The longing.

She cried out, rising against him, but then he moved slowly no longer. A whirlwind swept around them. Magical, wonderful. She was aware of the cool feel of the air around them, because her flesh was on fire. She was soaring upward, but she keenly felt the softness of the comforter brushing against her flesh. She rose to some distant plain with him...

But she was so aware of his body. His thighs, so rough against her own, muscled, huge, taut. His belly, flat, damp, teasing her with every brush, every stroke and movement. His fingers, his hands...now at the side of her head, for anything held back was unleashed, and a sweet rhythm was rushing by faster and faster. Wonder filled her again and again, rising. Going even higher. She met his eyes, then she cried out, startled, almost frightened by the volatility of the sweet climax that seized hold of her. She closed her eyes against his, suddenly, ridiculously shy. She wound her arms around his neck, turning her face to the side and holding tight to him. Then she felt a great quaking within his shoulders, a stiffening like rock, and then a slow relaxation. Hot mercury seemed to fill her body.

He held deadly taut for what seemed like forever, then he slowly eased himself down beside her.

Neither of them spoke. He held her easily within his arms, and still the seconds ticked by. Hot, damp flesh cooled in the spring mountain air.

Then he gently ran his fingers over her shoulder. "I told you that I'd see you again," he reminded her.

Julie smiled. He had banished any discomfort she might have felt over her more than abandoned behavior.

"Yes, you did. You must be psychic."

It was the wrong thing to say. She felt the tension snake into his body, and it wasn't a sexual tension. He didn't exactly toss her away from him, but she felt him withdraw. Confused, hurt, she determined to draw away herself. Blindly she groped for something to cover herself with so that she could walk to the shower. There wasn't anything there. Her discarded clothing had gone flying and he was halfway lying on the comforter.

She didn't need anything. That would be like closing the barn door after the cow had run away, she reminded herself dryly. She just needed to leap up proudly and stride for the shower.

A long, tightly muscled arm fell over her. She couldn't hide forever. She met his eyes, a steady gray now, hard on hers.

"Julie," he said huskily, "I don't suppose I ever told you this. I really think you're the most beautiful woman I've ever met."

She was going to melt. She had to take great care. She sometimes felt as if she was dealing with Dr. Jeykll and Mr. Hyde. "That isn't necessary now, McCoy, is it? We've been where you wanted to go."

His brow flew up incredibly and he was suddenly sitting, staring her down.

She wasn't going to be intimidated. It was time to make that proud march into the shower. She stood up. "Yes, excuse me—"

He stood and blocked her path. He didn't seem at all alarmed at his own nudity.

It alarmed Julie.

She had more time to look at him now. And she certainly had a more complete picture.

Her knees were weak all over again. She really did like everything about him. Even his arrogance. He was standing there with his hands on his hips, the breadth of his shoulders very straight, and the whole of him seeming to tick and pulse with tension once again. Bronze, taut and big. She felt her palms going damp and her eyes drawn just where they shouldn't be.

He smiled suddenly. "Yeah. I got what I wanted. Like you weren't ready to jump my bones, Miss Hatfield."

"If you will just excuse me—" she said again, trying to stride imperiously by him.

It wasn't easy. He caught her by the shoulders and swung her around. And she struggled and started to shout out a real protest but she never found her voice. He was kissing her again. That same kind of kiss that seemed to bathe all her insides, that had gotten them here to begin with.

She pulled away from him determinedly. "I'm taking a shower, McCoy."

She moved quickly, before he could stop her again, her mind in a whirl. What was it with him? There were moments when they seemed so close.

Moments when it seemed as if he was a lover she might have waited a lifetime to meet.

And then . . .

Then something leaped up between them. A wall, a barrier, as cold, as hard as stone.

She was still a charlatan. Sweet and simple.

That thought gave her the strength to slip by him to her bathroom.

Once the bathroom had been a bedroom. Julie had always wanted a huge bathroom. One with double sinks and a separate shower and tub, and she'd been determined that the tub would be huge and deep and have a nice hot whirlpool in it. Once she had saved enough of the money she received from the sale of her short stories, she had invested it immediately in her bathroom. It was a wonderful place.

But she didn't give it the least heed as she marched in, slammed the door and slipped into the glass-enclosed shower. She jerked the water on. It came out freezing cold. So cold that she gave a little scream, then stood beneath it anyway. Maybe it was exactly what she needed.

Suddenly the glass door opened. McCoy was right behind her.

"What the hell happened?"

She stared at him blankly, water dripping over her eyes.

"You screamed."

"Oh! The water. It was cold."

"That's all?" he demanded incredulously.

"Well, I didn't mean to scream. It was just cold."

McCoy was wet now, too, with the water spraying over his naked body.

"Move over, Hatfield," he said softly.

"I will not—" she began, but he was already inside the shower stall and closing the door behind him. He stepped behind Julie, then reached over her shoulder to adjust the temperature. The water became much warmer quickly.

She felt his hands, slick with soap, on her back. "Julie, I meant what I said."

"What?"

She knew what he had said. She just wanted to hear it again.

"That you're beautiful," he said softly. "Really beautiful. So small...so delicate..." His soapy fingers accentuated his words, sensually moving against her shoulders and spine, curving and finding the pattern of muscles and bones. "So damned...perfect." The whisper came against the lobe of her ear. And as he whispered, his hands moved around, slipping and rubbing over her breasts and belly, and below.

"McCoy," she protested, turning in his arms. Her eyes widened as she seemed to fit right against the renewed arousal of his body.

Then she found herself pressed against the wall of the shower stall with the water hot and rushing over them. She kissed his soaking chest, tasting the salt of the man and the heat of the water.

And as it rained down around them, he made love to her once again.

The water turned cold. They were still entwined, still breathing heavily and still leaning against the wall. McCoy swore beneath his breath.

"What kind of a hot water tank do you keep?" he demanded.

"Well, we have been in here a very long time," Julie reminded him.

He shut off the water and pushed open the door, snaking a towel quickly off the rack to wrap her in before finding one for himself. She watched him curiously as his eyes met hers again at last.

"Do you or do you not like me, McCoy?" she asked frankly.

A handsome smile curved his lips. "Obviously, I like you, Miss Hatfield."

"Then why do you suddenly get so mad at me all the time?"

"Because I don't want to hear about this ridiculous psychic business!"

"Ridiculous?" Julie said. He didn't answer. His jaw was set in that line again. The barrier was up. Hot and cold.

She swung around and walked to her room. She ignored him as she dug into her drawers for clothing, choosing jeans and a T-shirt. He watched her as she dressed, seeming to be in no hurry to do so himself. Then he suddenly strode across the room and gripped her shoulders.

"Julie, damn it, we both knew we were coming to this. You are beautiful. I have never wanted anyone more. And it's more than wanting...it's your eyes. It's your voice. It's the way that you care about people.

Hell, yes, I like you. I just don't want to hear about the voodoo bit when we're together!"

She pulled back, staring at him. "You say that you care about me, McCoy. But don't you see? It's part of what I am! I can't take it on and off like a coat!"

"What do you mean, it's part of what you are?" he demanded. His voice was rough and angry. "That's it, that's your whole function, your life?"

"You're a G-man, right?"

"That's a job, Julie. It's what I do for a living."

She sighed softly. "And you do it day and night."

"I don't—"

"But you do. It's not just a job to you, it's more. If you're needed at night, you're there. I wouldn't ask you to change."

"It's not the same at all! Unless you're trying to tell me that you do this for a living—"

"No!" Julie said. "I would never charge anyone to help them. I've never taken a penny and I wouldn't. There's no way to put a price on human life."

His jaw was still at that angle that meant trouble.

"No tea leaves during the week, no crystal balls?"

She gritted her teeth, spun around and hurried down the stairs, leaving him behind.

From the main hallway she walked through the formal dining room to the kitchen. She was muttering beneath her breath as she filled the teakettle.

"Tea leaves, my foot!"

She slammed the kettle on the stove. When she turned around he was behind her again, barefoot and bare-chested.

And he didn't have a single problem making himself completely at home in her kitchen. He opened her refrigerator.

"I'm making tea," she said.

"Thanks, I'll have a beer." He found one, flipped the pop top and grimaced at her. "You're driving me to drink. What have you got to eat?"

"We just came from brunch."

He looked at his watch. "That was five hours ago."

"You're kidding!" Julie gasped, glancing at her watch. He wasn't kidding. And she was suddenly starving.

"Haven't you got anything in here that isn't green?"

"I do not have molded food in my refrigerator!"

"No, but the only thing you do have seems to be lettuce."

"Well, it isn't," Julie said indignantly. She came to the refrigerator and pushed him aside.

Maybe tea wasn't the right idea at exactly this moment after all. She had a chilled bottle of white Zinfandel, which she set on the counter with a bang, then she opened the freezer. He had simply been looking in the wrong place. She had lots of food. Chicken, lamb, pork, beef. She even had a turkey. Microwave defrostable? She had to stick with the beef.

"Is stir-fry too avant-garde for you?"

"I do stretch to a bit more than meat and potatoes," he said. "Especially if you're cooking."

"We could call for a pizza with the works."

He grimaced. "Not on your life. Cook, woman."

She arched a warning brow. "You'd best be careful. You're coming very close to having a greasy pizza."

For some reason, she didn't mind the idea of cooking for him, although she should have minded. She tossed the package of sirloin strips into the microwave and dived into the green stuff in her refrigerator, some of which wasn't green at all. She had red bell peppers as well as green, and mushroom caps and onions.

"Should I pour you a glass of wine?" he asked her.

"Please."

She began chopping vegetables while he opened the wine bottle. She noted that he knew right where to go for the corkscrew, but she didn't comment on it because he didn't seem to realize it himself. And since she had already started chopping the vegetables, she didn't want to get into another of their arguments where he could either stalk out—or she could become determined to throw him out.

If she was capable of carrying out such a deed.

"So what do you do?" he asked her.

"What?"

"For a living. You said you aren't paid for being a—"

"Charlatan?" she asked sweetly. She pulled out the wok, then dug out her peanut oil and teriyaki and oyster sauces. "Well, I was left some money."

"Nice," he commented.

"No, not really. I'd much rather have my parents back."

"Sorry," he said softly. "I didn't mean it in that way. But does that mean that you're independently wealthy?"

She shook her head. "I write short stories."

"Really?" He poured her glass of wine, handed it to her and propped himself up on the counter with his beer to watch her. "What kind of short stories?"

"Charlatan short stories."

"Now really, the question was civil."

"By your standards, I imagine it was."

"Testy, testy."

"We charlatans get that way."

"Are you going to finish slicing that onion or do you need help? I'm hungry. Let's get going!"

She stared at him, amazed, then saw the silver glitter in his eyes and knew he was doing his best to get beneath her skin. "I think I'd rather do the chopping. And you're the guest. And not really invited. Therefore, you can just wait until I'm done."

"Just remember, I have to report to work in the morning."

Julie sipped her wine and looked at him. A sharp tremor seized her. Was he leaving the area already? She was startled by the sharpness of the pain that seized her. They were scarcely friends.

They were lovers.

And with her whole heart, she didn't want him to go.

"Here? Are you still working out of the station—or do you have to be back in Washington, or wherever it is that you usually do work?"

"No, I'm still working here," he said softly, the humor gone from his eyes as he studied the beer bottle. "Tracy Nicholson came out of it okay, and that was the most important thing. But we didn't catch our man."

"You think he'll strike again?"

"Yes."

Julie stared at her wok. There was a very frightening criminal out there. A kidnapper, a murderer.

And all she could think for the moment was that she was absurdly pleased McCoy wouldn't be leaving the area.

"Do you want—" she started to ask, then broke off. No, he wouldn't want her help.

"Do I want what?"

"Wine with dinner, or would you like another beer?"

"I'll have a glass of wine with you, if you don't mind making some coffee after."

Julie laughed softly.

"Coffee is funny?"

"Well, you found the beer yourself, managed to inveigle dinner—"

"And sex. Don't forget the sex."

Julie flushed. She hadn't forgotten it.

She never would.

"At any rate, I just can't imagine you asking for the coffee so politely. Not when you tend to see what you want and merely take it."

"Do I do that?"

"Yes."

"Did I do that with you?"

"Yes."

He grinned slowly in return. "Good. That means I can probably do it again."

"McCoy, damn you—"

"Your meat is sizzling," he told her. He leaped from the counter, still grinning. "Shall we eat?"

"I'm not so sure," Julie murmured. But he was already reaching for the plates he could see through the glass cabinet doors.

"I think we need to eat really quickly."

"Why?"

"Because we just might have another argument coming on. And your stir-fry smells delicious. And I'm starving. And I don't want you to throw me out of the house before I get a chance to wolf it all down."

Despite herself, Julie was smiling again.

How was it possible to want to hang a man one minute and find herself laughing the next?

Well, that was McCoy. He was complex and hard. Sometimes distant, and sometimes as weary as if he had already lived out a whole lifetime.

And then there were times like this. When his chest muscles gleamed like copper and his dark blond hair was still damp and falling disobediently over his forehead and one eye. When some of the silver edge had left his eyes, and he seemed so young, so handsome...

And so damned sexy...

"Yes! We need to eat. Quickly!" Julie said. She was not letting her mind wander in that direction again.

She scooped the concoction from the wok onto two plates.

"Where shall we eat?" McCoy asked.

"The dining room?"

"Too mundane."

"The kitchen?"

"Too tight. Ah," he said softly. "The bedroom?"

Julie shook her head warily. "Too intimate."

"Well, that was the idea."

"You have to work tomorrow," Julie reminded him. "Remember, you've got to get going. We'll eat in the parlor."

It would be safe, Julie thought.

But it wasn't.

McCoy just wasn't a safe man.

They dined slowly. They talked politely. Mostly about Brenda and her children. Julie learned that his brother-in-law was a serviceman based in D.C. but on loan to a base in California at the moment. Their conversation remained pleasant, easy, casual.

"I have to go," McCoy said softly. "Go—or stay," he added.

"Oh, no," Julie said. "Not tonight. You're not staying tonight. We hardly know one another."

"I thought we were getting acquainted rather well."

"No. You have to go," she said. But his eyes were on her lips. He watched her speak with fascination. He reached out and touched her lip gently with his fingertip.

"I'm going."

But he didn't leave. He pulled her into his arms again. His lips came down on hers. Tasting them, brushing them. Slowly, slowly savoring them.

Julie broke away, looking into his eyes. "You have to...to..."

Damn, but she liked his mouth. It was full and generous. And sensual. And when it met hers...as it was doing again...she felt such a startling arousal and sweet birth of emotion.

"I have to what?" he whispered softly. The warmth of his breath touched her ear. Seared her throat. Entered into her.

They hadn't had an argument for well over an hour, she realized.

She met his eyes, secure in the warmth of his arms, and she smiled. Slowly. Wickedly.

"You have to stay, McCoy. That's what you have to do."

He laughed softly.

And kissed her again.

Chapter 6

Julie hadn't expected to find herself at the police station the next morning, but by ten o'clock, that was exactly where she was.

And the man with whom she had shared a warm and passionate night was staring at her as if she was a distasteful stranger. A thunderous frown knotted his forehead, and his lips were drawn tight and thin.

It hadn't been Julie's idea to come. She had considered herself done with the case for now. She could help with the victim—not with the criminal.

But Petty had wanted her called in.

McCoy had left her house very early, just about with the crack of dawn. He'd gone home, showered, shaved and changed, and this morning, he looked just like a G-man.

He was wearing a three-piece suit.

And like black leather and casual knit shirts—and nothing at all—he wore it very well. The suit accentuated the tightly-muscled leanness of his physique and the breadth of his shoulders. His hair this morning was firmly brushed back from his forehead—the better to see the scowl, my dear, she thought—and he was all business.

Well, she wasn't particularly pleased about the turn of events herself. She had been so tired when he had left. Deliciously sleepy, worn and warm. She had barely roused herself when she'd heard him whisper that he was leaving and felt his kiss on her forehead. And when she had fallen asleep again, it had been a deep, comfortable sleep.

Then her doorbell had seemed to shrill with the force of a million banshees, and she had shot up, disoriented. The doorbell had continued that awful screeching as she promised herself that she was either going to get a new one or rip the entire thing out while she hopped around, quickly trying to drag on a pair of jeans so that she could answer the summons and make the noise stop.

Joe Silver and Patty had been on her porch. "Petty wants to see you, Julie. He said that we're not to let you escape. We're to sit right here until you're ready to go to the station."

"You're kidding," Julie told her.

"No. I'll make the coffee. Have you any of that mocha blend to grind? I love it. It tastes better at your house than any other place in the world."

"Thanks, yes, grind away," Julie called after her, looking at Joe Silver. He was a nice-looking man, midthirties, medium height and build, dark brown eyes, with a great smile. Julie had wondered for a long time if there wasn't something going on between him and Patty.

Patty always denied it.

"What does Petty want?" Julie asked Joe.

"He wants you to talk to a police artist from Charlestown, a man who's supposed to be one of West Virginia's finest."

"A police artist?"

"Yes. To give him a description."

"But a description of what? I didn't see anything!"

Joe shrugged. "Well, I told Petty that. He's just grasping at straws, but you know Petty when he gets something set in his mind."

"Yes, I know Petty."

"Coffee's on. Get ready, Julie," Patty said. "We're not allowed to let you dawdle."

"Does our G-man know I'm coming?" she asked, trying to keep her tone light.

"Yes, he knows," Joe told her. He was watching her closely. So was Patty. Had they both guessed that there was something going on between her and McCoy?

"And?"

"And what?" Patty demanded.

"He can't be pleased."

"Oh, he isn't," Patty assured her cheerfully, waving a dismissive hand in the air. "But it is Petty's station. And even our real McCoy respects that. Um, wake up and smell the coffee. Isn't that a great aroma?" she asked Joe. "I'll get you some. Julie Hatfield, you go get ready!"

So she'd gotten dressed, choosing a light knit business suit with a soft white lace-trimmed blouse beneath, and stockings, fully aware that she'd need to be composed around her doubting McCoy.

She hadn't quite expected the look she was getting from him now. He hadn't addressed her since she'd come into the station.

Now he was half leaning and half sitting on Petty's broad desk, his arms crossed, one long leg firmly on the floor, the other dangling. The police artist was sitting next to Julie, and Petty was in front of her, straddling an office chair and resting his chin on the high arched back of it as he watched Julie. Joe and Patty had been dismissed after bringing her in. Timothy Riker, the chief's right-hand man, was there, too.

If McCoy wasn't speaking to Julie at the moment, then Julie made sure she didn't have anything to say to him. She addressed Petty and the artist. "I didn't really see the man, Petty. If I'd had any kind of a picture, I would have told you. You know that."

"Yes, Miss Hatfield, but anything would be helpful at this point. Any impression at all. All I want you to do is close your eyes and think—and give me anything at all that comes into your mind."

Julie leaned forward, closing her eyes. At first she couldn't think at all.

McCoy had been staring at her with daggers in his eyes, and that made concentration hard. Even when she wasn't looking at him, she could feel the heat of his gaze.

Pity they didn't need a description of McCoy. She could have told them inch by inch exactly what he looked like, his face, his legs, his chest, his...

Shoulders...

No, she couldn't see the kidnapper's face. But she could see his shoulder.

Fear ripped through her, suddenly, vividly.

Then the visions rushed in upon her. She was with Tracy again. Tracy as she stood in the road, Tracy as the man jumped from the car to sweep her up.

Tracy, struggling...

She couldn't see the man's face. Couldn't see it at all because a stocking was pulled over it, distorting his features. But as Tracy fought with him, she pulled at his shirt. A long-sleeved tailored shirt. But he wasn't wearing a tie, and several buttons were undone.

Tracy ripped another one off. And the shirt slid off his shoulder. And there it was.

A scar. About three inches, jagged. Maybe it had come from a fall or a knife wound. At one time, the tear had been deep. And it had left behind that scar...

The same scar that Julie had seen in her dream. That dream she had nearly forgotten this morning, that dream in which her lover came to her...

She was trembling, yet she was achingly aware that she had been afraid the scar had belonged to her dream lover. And now she knew.

No, they were not one and the same.

And then the realization struck her. They were coming closer and closer to the time when the terror would not come to her through another.

The terror would be for her...

"Julie! Julie! Are you all right?"

Her eyes flew open. Petty was on his knees before her, grasping her hands. They were cold and clammy.

Timothy was standing right behind the chief, his eyes wide with alarm.

Even McCoy had jumped off his doubting perch on the desk. Julie stared at him and felt the remnants of her fear send chills dancing down her spine. I can't see you again, ever, she thought wildly.

But could that help her? Had what she had seen in that dream already been set into motion?

And were the feelings she had for McCoy stronger than fear...

Stronger than destiny.

"Julie?" Petty said anxiously.

"I—I'm all right. I'm sorry," she said. She looked at the artist. She shook her head. "Honestly, I can't help you. Tracy didn't see his face. All I can tell you is that he was wearing a stocking over his face, that he's probably about five feet ten inches, dark-haired—and that he has a scar, like a jagged knife scar, on his left shoulder."

She heard a soft explosion of sound.

McCoy. The sound was one that ridiculed her. Angrily.

He suddenly strode across the room, leaving the office. The door snapped sharply behind him.

"You're sure of this?" Petty asked her.

Julie nodded. "Petty, I've never been more sure."

Petty nodded and shrugged to the police artist. "That's about all we're going to get. Medium height, medium build, darkish hair."

"And that scar," Timothy said.

"Yeah, the scar," Petty said. "Too bad it isn't on our fellow's face. It might be kind of hard walking around trying to get the populace to bare their shoulders."

Julie grimaced. "I'm sorry."

"You've given us plenty, Julie. Thanks," Petty told her.

She nodded and started out. "Tracy is doing fine, right?" she asked Petty.

"Tracy is doing wonderfully," Petty told her. "No problems at all. It's great to be young, huh?"

"Probably. I don't remember."

"Ah, you're just a babe yourself, Julie Hatfield. Wait till you reach my age, then you'll know!"

She smiled and turned to leave.

McCoy was sitting on the corner of Patty's desk in the outer office. He was glaring at her, a deep frown imbedded in his forehead. Patty had moved to Timothy Riker's desk and had her nose stuck in her typing. Joe Silver was trying to look every bit as busy, going through the files.

Everyone was aware that there was a storm brewing here, and everyone seemed determined to avoid it.

Well, there wasn't even going to be a raindrop, Julie decided. She smiled pleasantly, gave an easy wave to Patty and Joe and walked out of the building.

That was when she remembered she had been driven in by Patty and Joe.

Well, hell! She had made it out so smoothly. She didn't feel like ruining her fine exit by going back.

She gritted her teeth as she stood there. Then the door opened behind her and she knew it was him. "Come on," he said curtly. "I'll get you home."

It would be rather futile to argue. It was a long walk.

But still, even as she crawled into the Lincoln and he sat down beside her, she felt as if she were next to dynamite about to explode.

"All right, McCoy, just what is your problem?" she demanded.

"Nothing. Nothing! I have no problems, Miss Hatfield. It's just that we have a psychic here, but funny, she can't give us a description of a man—"

"He was wearing a stocking!"

"He's of medium height and medium build and probably dark haired. Well, let's see. That probably describes half the men in the immediate area. Hell, it describes half of the men in our law-enforcement agencies!"

"It lets out Petty," Julie remarked coolly.

"That's right, it does. And thank God, my hair is fairly light, so maybe it lets me out, too. Except maybe not. After all, you did ask me if I had a scar on my shoulder."

Julie stiffened, remembering the occasion. Yes, she had asked him! Because she had seen the scar. She had seen it in the dream, and he had been in the dream. And she had been left to wonder...

But she knew now that he was the man in her dream. The lover in her dream.

But he was not the man who brought the awful, shattering sense of danger...

"You did ask me about a scar, Julie!"

"Yes."

"Yet it seemed in the office just now as if you were seeing that scar on the kidnapper for the first time."

Damn, he was still so angry! Well, maybe it did look as if she was a charlatan.

"I just saw the scar through Tracy's eyes in the office," she said. He was never going to understand. He didn't believe in her to begin with.

"Where did you see it before?"

"In a—dream."

"A nightmare, huh? And I was in it, right? Before or after we met?"

There was a tight note of sarcasm edging his voice.

Julie sat back, gritting her teeth. "If you recall, McCoy, you didn't answer me about whether you did or didn't have a scar."

"That's right, I didn't, did I? Is that why we made love? Were you checking out my shoulder?"

"Oh, McCoy, you are really something, do you know that? A true prize!" Julie exclaimed furiously. "Stop the car. I'd rather walk."

He wouldn't stop the car. She knew that.

But he did stop it. He pulled abruptly off the road onto the narrow shoulder and turned to her with a sudden, startling passion. "Did you check out my shoulder? Did you check it out really well? Did you think long and hard about what you were doing?"

Had she thought long and hard? No, she hadn't thought for a single second.

But she knew his shoulders bore no scars. She knew simply because she had been so fascinated by his body, by every minute stretch of bronze flesh.

"McCoy, obviously, neither one of us gave it long, hard thought, or else last night would have never happened! And it's probably best if we pretend that it never did happen. And if you don't mind—"

She started to reach for the door. If he really meant to let her out on the side of the road, then she'd just get out on the side of the road.

"What do you think you're doing?" he demanded.

"I'm getting out."

"Here?"

"Well, you stopped."

He exploded with an oath. The Lincoln suddenly roared to life.

He didn't speak again until they were in front of her house. Then he leaned over and opened the passenger door for her. "Julie, you go ahead and get as mad at me as you want to, but don't you suppose that you'd better start thinking?"

"What are you talking about now?"

"You don't ever just get out on the side of the mountain and start walking. And you don't leave your doors open, and you take care when you're alone."

Her heart suddenly slammed against her chest. "Why?"

Was he worried? Did he think that just maybe his nephew had been right? That the kidnapper knew about her, that he had worn the stocking over his face because he knew that Julie might be called in on the case?

"Because every woman in this area is at risk right now, Julie. You can't behave foolishly."

She remembered the force of her dream. Yes, she had been in danger. But the danger had involved him.

She just needed not to see him again. That was all. And she would be all right. Since he was so angry, so disgusted, that should be easy.

"I'll be careful," she told him, slipping out of his car.

The Lincoln remained parked in front of her house until she let herself in and locked the door.

"He's angry. He won't come back," she whispered.

But he would come back.

She could refuse to see him.

But already, an ache was growing in her heart. She didn't want him out of her life. She wanted him back, now. She wanted to sleep beside him again through the night. She wanted to go on discovering more about him. She wanted to go on . . .

Falling in love with him. A little bit more every day. Needing him as badly as she wanted him.

"Destiny is not preset!" she announced aloud. He wasn't the man she wanted or needed in her life. Once before, she had fallen in love with a doubting Thomas.

With tragic consequences. From every single direction, it was better to stop this now.

Three days later, when Julie had convinced herself that he wasn't going to return to her life, McCoy appeared on her front doorstep.

It was early, barely eight in the morning. No dream or inner sense had warned her that he might appear.

She had finally begun to work last night on a story for a mystery magazine and she had stayed up very late.

When the doorbell rang she barely managed to find an old terry robe and wrap it around her long johns and stumble down the stairs.

And stupidly, she threw the door open without glancing through the peephole, without even pausing to wonder who it might be.

"What in God's name do you think you're doing?"

That was McCoy's greeting.

He was freshly showered and shaved, and she could smell the faint and pleasant aroma of his after-shave. His hair was slicked back, still damp from the shower. But he wasn't wearing his three-piece suit today. He was very casual, wearing cutoff denims and an old football jersey and sneakers that had a few holes in the toes.

Julie stepped back, rubbing her forehead. "Answering my door."

"What did I tell you the last time I saw you?"

"McCoy—"

"Julie, damn it—"

"I saw you through the peephole—"

"You're lying!"

"How the hell would you know?" she demanded. But he did know. Was it because of the expression on her face, or was it maybe true that McCoy did have a hint of second sight of his own?

"Okay, I forgot. I was working last night—"

"No good, Julie."

"Okay! I'll be more careful in the future, I promise. What do you want, McCoy, or did you come over just to torture me?"

"No." He hesitated a minute, then sighed. "I was at a standstill. Getting nowhere. I thought some time off might help. I came to take you out."

She arched her brows, a smile curving her lip as she stared at him from head to toe, indicating his outfit. "Out? Where?"

"Tubing."

"Tubing?" Then she looked past him to his car. Three heavy black tire tubes were strapped on top of the elegant Lincoln.

"Are you game?" he asked her.

"Well, you know, McCoy, I might be working. Or I might have had other plans for the day—"

"Oh, you did not. You told Patty you might go to a movie with her tomorrow night, and if you worked till the wee hours last night, I don't think that you're going to slam right back into it this morning."

"As a matter of fact—"

"Yes?"

She had been going to work. She had proofed her story last night—all she needed was a clean copy. "Can you give me thirty minutes?"

"I can give you a couple of hours. The sun will be stronger by then."

"All right. Can we run by the post office?"

"Anywhere you want."

"All right. You're on then. Make yourself at home. I'll hurry."

Julie suspected that he might follow her up the stairs and into the shower, but he didn't.

She was alarmingly disappointed. She dressed quickly in a bathing suit, T-shirt and shorts and managed to find a pair of sneakers just as full of holes as the pair he was wearing.

When she hurried downstairs, the coffee was ready, and he had toasted several English muffins.

"Thanks," Julie told him, biting into one and pouring herself a cup of coffee. He was on the back porch, at the round wooden table, sipping coffee, reading the paper and looking over the hills and valleys. He looked up, nodded and smiled, and looked back to his paper. "Go ahead. Go to work. You don't need to worry about entertaining me."

She didn't worry about him. She took her coffee and muffin into the office behind the parlor on the left side of the house and sat down. She concentrated on making her changes, then sighed with satisfaction as she sat back, delighted with the way that things had fallen into completion. After she turned on her printer, she wandered into the kitchen for a second cup of coffee.

McCoy was still on the porch, still looking over the mountains. Julie felt a soft warmth steal over her.

There were so many things against them. One of them being the way he felt about her second sight—or whatever he wanted to call it.

But there was something nice between them that she hadn't realized until then. They were both mountain lovers. They loved this region. They loved the foliage and the greenery, and the hills and the curves. They loved the way the sun rose here, and the way it set. They loved the quiet, and the serenity.

She hadn't made a sound. He turned suddenly, and Julie knew he had been aware she was there.

"How's it going?" he asked her.

"Fine. I'm just about done."

"Whenever. Let me know."

Julie went into her house and sipped the rest of her coffee while the printer finished throwing out her pages.

He did know how to make himself at home here. He'd been into the various bags of coffee beans she kept in the freezer, studying and selecting his choices.

She had a tendency to add heavily on the various flavors, like cinnamon or nut, while McCoy, she was learning, liked a stronger basic blend of coffee with just a hint of flavor.

Opposite ends of a pole, she reminded herself.

But then, opposites did attract.

Julie let out a sigh of exasperation with herself, collected her long line of paper from the printer and began to tear at the perforations, creating a neat little stack of manuscript. She dug out an envelope, quickly addressed it and hurried from her office.

She certainly hadn't had any bad dreams about tubing down the river. And the weather was beautiful; the day ahead looked bright.

"All set?" he asked her when she appeared in the kitchen.

"All set. Where are we starting from?" she asked him, as they left the house together.

"Maryland side," he said, frowning at her as he slipped on his sunglasses.

"What now?" Julie asked.

"The door. You didn't lock the door."

Julie exhaled slowly and hurried back to lock her front door. "Well, it's your fault, you know. You're so willing to jump down my throat all the time, I must be thinking inwardly that I need to give you a good reason to do so."

"Right."

Julie walked by him to the car. She smiled when she saw the ice chest wedged into the one tube. "What are we bringing with us?"

"A fine, vintage Bordeaux, how's that sound?"

"Elegant."

"Well, I'm afraid that it goes with unelegant cold fried chicken, potato salad, slaw and chips."

Julie grinned. "It will do."

The conversation was easy and light enough while he drove to their point of debarkation. It was public ground, not a spot owned by any of the rafting companies. While McCoy brought the tubes down, Julie watched him. She grabbed the first one as he tossed it her way.

"Hey, McCoy!"

"What?"

"Tubing down with the current is going to be great. How are we getting back to the car?"

He walked up to her and tweaked her cheek. Since she was balancing two tubes, she had no power to stop him. "Oh, ye of little faith!" he said. "I have a friend who has a little coffee spot almost right on the water some miles down from here. By then we'll have something warm like chocolate or coffee and tea, and then he or one of his kids will drive us to the car. How does that sound?"

"Great. Let's get started," Julie said. She stripped off her T-shirt and shorts then flushed as she realized McCoy was staring at her. She had worn what she thought was a fairly demure bathing suit. It was one piece and black, but the French cut rode high on her thighs, and the back was very low, falling an inch beyond her waist.

He wolf whistled. She wasn't sure whether to thank him or slap him.

She threw her shirt at him. "You've seen me in less."

"Yes, but I'm afraid to bring you in front of others in that getup. They might want to see you in less, too."

"McCoy—"

"Don't worry, Miss Hatfield. We McCoys are the proprietarial type. No one would dare come near, I promise. Want to throw the shorts over?"

She did so, then she decided that she had to hand it to McCoy—he really was prepared. He had a waterproof sack for them to stuff their shirts and her shorts into, and then a place to set the sack on a wire shelf in the cooler. He had a thin rope to connect the cooler tube with his own tube, and while Julie touched the water—letting out a yelp as its spring freshness touched her skin—McCoy was managing as only a man who had grown up playing with tubes on rivers could do. He was all set and ready while she was still wincing.

"I thought you grew up here!" he called to her. "Come on, get a move on!"

"Well, the water just wasn't quite this cold when I was younger," Julie assured him. She settled into her tube despite the cold washing over her. "And I did grow up here. And I've tubed this very water eighteen trillion times."

"Eighteen trillion?" McCoy said, grinning broadly.

She smiled, glad that she had come with him, wondering how she had managed to get through the days when he hadn't appeared.

Don't, don't, don't fall in love, she warned herself. But she was too late. It was already happening.

She was comfortable in her tube at last, accustomed to the water. A surge came rushing by her, lifting her along. Her feet trailed over the muddy and rocky bottom, but her hole-filled sneakers protected her feet. White caps lifted her over a smooth rapid in the way, bringing her tube crashing against McCoy's.

"Hey!"

"Oh, buck up!" Julie retorted. "There's calmer water ahead."

His arm snaked out, and his hand caught her wrist. For a moment their tubes twirled in a wide circle through the water, then they reached a patch of calm past the rocks, in the high water. He smiled and leaned back but didn't release her. Julie closed her eyes and felt the sun on her face.

She was quiet for a moment, then she asked him, "Why did you come back today?"

He didn't move. He was stretched comfortably, basking in the sun. "I wanted to see you."

"But nothing has changed about me," she reminded him quietly. "I'm still a charlatan."

She saw his jaw harden. "If only we didn't have to talk about it all the time—"

"But trying to pretend—"

"Julie, it's a beautiful day. Do we have to go through this?"

She gritted her teeth and closed her eyes. A sudden flash of sight came to her, and she smiled. "All right,

McCoy. In a matter of minutes, we're going to pass by a large rock in the middle of the river. And there's going to be a big black snake sitting on it, sunning itself."

"Oh, yeah?"

"Yeah!"

Julie was right. They came upon the snake just a few minutes later.

"Don't you see?" she pleaded. "I do know things sometimes. Not always, but sometimes."

McCoy was silent.

"Well? What do you think now?" Julie persisted.

"I think you bribed the snake," he said very seriously.

"Oh, come on!"

"All right, Julie. Maybe you were out here a few weeks ago. Maybe you knew the rock was there. Maybe you didn't know that you knew the rock was there, the memory was just sitting there, somewhere in the back of your mind. And if there had been a snake on it before, why couldn't there be a snake there again?"

Julie groaned and leaned back again. The swirling waters brought them crashing together. Her leg brushed his.

"McCoy?" she asked softly.

"What?"

"If I asked you not to do something—if I were really passionate about it—would you listen to me?"

"Julie—"

"McCoy, please, this is important to me. If I sensed that you could be hurt...really hurt...would you listen?"

"Julie, you know how I—"

"Even if it was just to humor me?"

"Let's stop over there, on the rocks, and pull up the cooler."

"McCoy!" Julie snapped. But it didn't matter. He wasn't listening. The water was hip deep, and he'd slipped from his tube. He dragged the tube with the cooler along with him to where some high, flat rocks were rising out of the water.

Julie slipped from her tube, too, and followed him. By the time she dragged her tube beside his, he had opened the cooler and pulled out the bags of food.

"Have a seat, Miss Hatfield. Lunch is served."

Julie sighed and sat in the sun. It was high in the sky now, bright and warming. There was a soft breeze moving through the trees that lined the river bank. The water was so many colors, blue and green and aqua and white where it dashed over the rocks. The scenery was incredibly beautiful.

McCoy passed her a plastic picnic plate with chicken and little containers of potato salad and cole slaw. He sat beside her, munching a drumstick.

Julie glanced at him and felt a fierce pang in her heart as she studied him. She cared about him so much. From the hot steel in his gray and silver eyes to the tight cords and muscles of every inch of his body. Someone like this came by only once in a lifetime.

And still...

"Is lunch all right?"

"It's amazing. Especially for a single man."

"Single men are extremely inventive and imaginative," he informed her. He suddenly passed her the wine bottle. "My sister made the lunch," he admitted.

Julie laughed softly. "We're supposed to drink this great wine out of the bottle?"

"I packed the wine. Can't you tell? I forgot the glasses."

She smiled again, laughed and swallowed a sip of wine before turning to her chicken. She was amazed at the appetites they had built up, and they ate in a companionable silence, waving at times as other tubers and rafters passed by their spot on the rocks.

When the food was gone, McCoy stuffed their plates and garbage into the cooler, but he didn't seem to be in any hurry to leave. They stretched out on the rocks, feeling the sun. Julie closed her eyes. Then she realized that he was leaning on an elbow beside her, staring at her.

She gazed into his eyes.

"That suit should be illegal," he told her. His finger traced a pattern softly over her hip.

"McCoy—"

"You should be illegal. Damn it, Julie, you're just the very last thing I needed now in my life. If only you weren't so damned beautiful..."

He leaned over and kissed her gently. Julie swallowed as his lips parted from hers. His kiss had promised more. So much more.

And she wanted it all.

But the pain was suddenly with her. "Answer me, McCoy," she said.

"About what?" He hedged again.

ACCEPT FOUR BRAND-NEW

YOURS

We'd like to send you four free Silhouette novels, worth more than $13.00, to introduce you to the benefits of the Silhouette Reader Service. We hope your free books will convince you to subscribe, but that's up to you. Accepting them places you under no obligation to buy anything, but we hope you'll want to continue with the Reader Service.

So unless we hear from you, once a month we'll send you four additional Silhouette Intimate Moments® novels to read and enjoy. If you choose to keep them, you'll pay just $2.96* per volume—a saving of 33¢ each off the cover price. There is no charge for postage and handling. There are no hidden extras! And you may cancel at any time, for any reason, just by sending us a note or a shipping statement marked "cancel." You can even return any shipment to us at our expense. Either way, the free books and gifts are yours to keep!

ALSO FREE!

VICTORIAN PICTURE FRAME

This lovely Victorian pewter-finish miniature is perfect for displaying a treasured photograph—and it's yours *absolutely free*—when you accept our no-risk offer.

Perfect for a treasured photograph

Plus a FREE mystery Gift! follow instructions at right.

* Terms and prices subject to change without notice.
Sales tax applicable in NY.

She touched his cheek. "If I was really certain that you were in danger, would you listen to me? Please, Robert, it's important."

"Well, I'll be damned. You do know my first name."

"McCoy!"

He laughed softly, then his expression became very serious. He traced the fullness of her lip with his thumb. "All right, Julie. Yes. If you were really afraid. If only to humor you."

She smiled, content.

He leaned close to her. "It's getting kind of cool now, isn't it?"

"Maybe. Just a little."

"I know how to get warmed up."

"Do you?"

He nodded gravely. "Come home with me, Miss Hatfield. I'll show you how."

She smiled and nodded. "Yes. I'll come home with you. And you can show me how."

•

Chapter 7

"Where is your home?" Julie asked, after McCoy's friend Jim Preston had taken them from the coffee shop, where she and McCoy had hot chocolate, to McCoy's car. She'd been somewhat surprised to discover that Jim's coffee shop was in the central Harpers Ferry area, one of the quaint and rustic eateries that catered to tourists.

She knew Jim Preston herself, if only casually. Like her and McCoy, Preston was a native of the area. He was a handsome man of medium height and build with dark sandy hair and dimples when he smiled.

Julie liked Jim and his two teenage children, and she was impressed with the warmth he and McCoy seemed to share. They were very old friends.

"I wonder why you and I never met before," Julie mused out loud, not realizing that she hadn't waited for an answer to her first question.

McCoy grinned, casting her a quick glance. "Well, Madam Curiosity, I imagine that the answers are the same to both questions. My mountain is on the Maryland side of the region."

She arched a brow. They had dropped his sister off near Charlestown on Sunday, and that was West Virginia, near the sight where Old John Brown had been hanged.

"My sister's home is new, remember. I still have the old family home in the hills, Miss Hatfield."

"Oh," she said, smiling. And then she waited, intrigued.

"Actually, I hadn't opened it up in years," he said softly. "My sister and Jim had painters in and got the place cleaned up when they heard that I was coming in from Washington. I hadn't thought I wanted to go back. But I've loved it since I've been here."

"Are your folks—gone?" Julie asked.

He smiled. "Gone to St. Petersburg. I bought this house from them when they moved. They didn't want to keep it, but they didn't want to let it out of the family, and at one time..." His voice drifted for a moment.

"At one time?" Julie persisted.

He shrugged. "It's a big place. Too big for them to keep up anymore. They've had it with ice and snow, and the only thing they say they really miss are the kids. That's not really true, though. They come back every year. Can't keep old mountaineers away from the mountains once it really turns to spring and summer."

"That's nice," Julie murmured. He hadn't said what he had been about to say.

He closed off frequently, she realized. There was something there that he didn't talk about. Or something that he didn't trust her enough to talk about yet.

She made a mental note to call his sister and see if they couldn't meet for lunch one afternoon. She had the feeling that McCoy's sister might be willing to tell her lots of things she wanted to know.

He turned up one of the old dirt mountain trails and the Lincoln began to climb in earnest. They moved through a deep forest area that was richly and heavily treed, and then the clearing with the house on it seemed to burst out in front of them.

It was stunning. Made of a rich dark wood that had been kept to natural shades, the house was as old or older than Julie's own family home, built big and broad, with wide, embracing porches. Four gables adorned the upstairs windows, while the back porch, enclosed by glass, seemed to jut over the mountain peak and look down on the beauty of the valley.

"Wow!" Julie said softly. She looked at McCoy. "This is some family home."

He shrugged. "My great-grandfather was a senator from the region, a man with a great dynasty in mind. Life is fickle, though. He had only one son, and that one son had only one son, my dad."

"Poor man," Julie said.

"He was probably the one who started the feud with the Hatfields," McCoy said lightly. "I hear that he was a very cantankerous old man. Maybe he started a feud with my great-grandmother, too. That would explain things."

"Was there really a feud, do you think?"

"Well, we seem proof of that, don't you think?"

"Maybe," Julie said, but she was still smiling.

"I love the house, though. I always have. It was a great place to grow up. Come on in."

Julie's smile deepened and she hurried out of the car and ran up the steps to the house. McCoy opened the front door, and they entered a great room with naked oak beams. It was full of overstuffed furniture and bookshelves, a warm, delightful and inviting room.

"This is the best," McCoy advised her, lifting a hand to indicate that she should pass through an arched opening to the back of the house.

Here was the porch that extended over the back. At one end of it was a massive fireplace that stretched from wall to wall. Before it was a large, thick fur rug, and just beyond the rug, close to where a blaze would flame, was a setting of furniture, an older wicker sofa and matching chairs and occasional tables. A comforter had been tossed over the back of the sofa.

At the other end was a very modern entertainment center. There was a table and chairs set out, and Julie quickly imagined that this was where McCoy came mornings.

Then she glanced at the thick fur rug and the comforter again, and she smiled. This was his favorite room. It was where he came to sleep. It wasn't because of the fireplace, it was because of the view of the sloping, forested fall to the valley deep below. A bubbling stream could be seen rushing down the mountain. The trees and bushes waved softly in the spring breeze, so deeply green, alive in shades of forest and kelly and the lightest of limes.

Julie inhaled softly and walked across the room to better see the view. McCoy stepped past her and slid open one of the windows. The soft, cool mountain breeze swept in around her. It touched her cheeks. It gently ruffled her hair.

"Like it?"

"I love it."

"Want something? Coffee, wine, water, anything? How about an Irish coffee? I think I have a can of whipped spray stuff in the fridge, I had the kids up here last night."

Julie smiled, feeling him beside her, but still stared at the view. "Irish coffee with whipped spray stuff sounds great."

"Don't make fun of my culinary talents," he warned her sternly.

"I wouldn't dream of it. You make wonderful coffee," she assured him as he left for the kitchen.

His view was even more spectacular than her own. She certainly didn't want to tell a McCoy that his mountain was better than hers, but it was an awfully pretty mountain.

Night was coming now. Here, up high and almost in the clouds, it came very evidently, and with an even greater array of color. She could still see the sun in the western sky, a brilliant orange, emitting streaks of that same shade across the sky. In places, the orange was tempered by a softer yellow, and down by the trees there seemed to be a darkening frame of shadows in shades of violet and purple.

He came gently into the room. She didn't so much hear him come as she sensed him. But she knew that he was with her.

She still looked out the window, looking at the extravagant colors, the sheer richness of spring. She felt the breeze. It moved through her hair, caressing her throat and her neck, touching her cheeks as gently as the soft movement of invisible fingers.

He was with her. She still hadn't heard his movement. She just knew. And she knew the scent of him. Subtle, masculine.

A slow, burning warmth began to fill her. Just because he was near.

Because he would touch her.

She knew the touch, and she knew the tenderness. She knew him, knew the man and knew things about him that made her love him. She didn't need to see him to know the contours of his face, the deep sandy shade of his hair, the compelling steel and silver of his eyes. She didn't need to see him to know the generous fullness of his mouth, the sensuality.

She knew all the hues within his heart and soul and mind, and those colors were all beautiful, and part of the warmth that touched her.

He could move so silently...

He would be coming across the room to her.

Yes, now.

A smile curved her lip.

He was coming closer and closer. Moving with long strides but silent grace. She felt him, and felt cocooned in the special warmth that he brought, felt a supreme sense of well-being come over her.

He was going to make love to her. Now. Prove that he knew exactly how to warm her.

He stood behind her and swept the fall of her hair from her neck, and she felt the wet, hot caress of his lips against her nape.

The pleasure was startling. So startling. Hot tremors swept instantly along her spine. Danced there. Her knees grew weak as swift-flowing desire came cascading into the depths of her being.

He held her hair, and his kiss skimmed over her shoulder. As he kissed her, he lifted the shoulder of her T-shirt. The soft knit slid from her shoulders. It fell to the floor in a pool of lilac. The feel as it left her flesh was so sensual. Soft, warm, exquisite, leaving her skin bared to his kiss.

The straps of her suit fell from her shoulders. The dampness of it peeled from her body, leaving more skin bared. Sensitive. Waiting.

She felt his hands on the snap of her shorts. She heard the long rasp of the zipper. The flutter of fabric as they fell. Then the coolness of her still-wet suit slid against her, landing discarded at her feet.

His arms encircled her. She could feel the strength of his naked chest as he pulled her against him. He still wore his cutoffs.

She could feel the roughness of the fabric against her tender skin. Even that touch was sensual.

His whisper touched her ear. The words, each breath of air, brought aching new sensation. "You are...exquisite. You do things to me that I hadn't imagined could be done..."

A smile curved her lips. She turned in the circle of his arms.

She stared up into his eyes and felt the driving passion in their silver depths.

And then he kissed her.

And she felt an explosion deep within her. She felt the hungry pressure of his lips, forming over her own, firmly, demandingly, causing them to part for the exotic presence of his tongue.

He'd kissed her before...

Never quite like this.

And when his lips left her mouth, they touched her throat. Touched the length of it. The soft, slow, sensual stroke of his tongue just brushing her flesh. With ripples of silken, liquid fire. She could see his hands, broad, so darkly tanned, upon the paleness of her skin. His fingers were long, handsomely tapered, callused, but with neatly clipped nails. Masculine hands. Hands that touched with an exciting expertise. Fingers that stroked with confidence and pleasure.

She allowed her head to fall back, her eyes to close. The sensations to surround her.

The breeze...it was so cool against her naked body. So soft. So unerringly sensual. Perhaps because her body was so hot. Growing fevered. But the air...it touched her where his kiss left off, and both fire and ice seemed to come to her and dance through her.

She spun in his arms. It was no longer daytime. Shadows were falling, and the breeze was growing cooler.

And his kiss went lower.

And where his lips touched her, she burned.

And where his lips had lingered earlier, the cool air stroked her with a sensuality all its own.

And still his kiss lowered. And lowered until he teased the base of her spine. And his hand caressed her naked buttocks and hips, and she was turning in his arms.

Her hand rested on his head, her breath quickened, and caught, and quickened again. She cried out, amazed at the tempest that rose within her, startled by the sheer sensual pleasure that ripped through her.

She cried out again, and again, and then discovered that she was sinking, sinking into his arms...

Night had come. The moon remained in the sky, but she could not see clearly.

Darkness was falling over the mountains. She reached out and touched his face, stroked the contours of his cheek. She pressed her lips against his, then against his forehead, then against each cheek. She groaned softly, kissing his throat, just teasing it with the barest brush of her teeth.

It was incredible to touch him. She was in his arms, and she was barely aware that they moved. Then they were sinking once again, down, deep, deep down into the fur before the fireplace.

She touched him then, again and again. Touched him, knowing the living warmth and fire of him. Feeling the ripple of muscle in his chest. Feeling his hands. Feeling the pulse of his body. Feeling... him.

It was so good to be with him. Life, feeling, sensation, all were so wonderfully vivid.

In the shadows he rose above her for a moment. Once again, she found that even sound could be scintillating as the quick rasp of his zipper tore against the silence of the darkened night.

She stretched out her arms, and he came down with her. He came down silently, gracefully. He braced himself over her, and then she cried out softly, wanting him so badly.

And finally having him.

She could feel him entering her...

The fur touched her back. She felt the softness, and the roughness. Her hands splayed over his chest, and she felt the rigor of his muscle, the exciting, slick feel of his bronze chest. In the near darkness, she could see his eyes, nearly a pure silver now, all sizzle and passion.

She could feel...

Movement. Slow, sure, then subtle, the pace quickening. Each stroke, faster, the rhythm growing. The wonder inside of her growing as his body touched hers, and touched it... inside and out.

She watched his eyes. Watched his tension, and watched his smile.

His lips touched down on hers. Took them hungrily, passionately, while his body filled hers.

She closed her eyes, but even in the darkness it seemed that stars suddenly burst in the middle of the heavens, like the births of a thousand suns. She quivered like a bow strung too tight, and then she catapulted into a sweet recess where wonder and magic all seemed to crash down upon her.

His arms were suddenly laced around her, tight. Great shudders racked the whole of his body, and the length of him came against her tautly. Then his arms eased, and he whispered something erotic in her ear and fell by her side. He lay there a second before sweeping her into his arms, his kiss brushing her forehead.

Silently, she curled against him. She wasn't going home. Not tonight. They both knew it. She let her fingers play over the crisp hairs on his chest. A wonderful warmth came slowly sweeping over her again.

It was so damned good to lie with him. There was such a sense of comfort and security here.

"Hey," he said softly.

"Hmm?"

"You're falling asleep."

"Am I? I'm just so comfortable."

"What about the coffee?"

"Um," she murmured. She didn't want any coffee. She didn't want to move. She didn't even want McCoy talking.

She felt too relaxed, too happy. And so wonderfully drowsy.

She didn't want to feud.

Neither did McCoy, it seemed. He wasn't moving.

"Will we burn the house down if we don't go for the coffee?" she whispered.

"No. It has an automatic turnoff."

"Good," Julie breathed softly. She closed her eyes. It had been a long day. Tubing... and now.

She must have drifted off to sleep, because she was quickly dreaming.

And it was so strange, for in her dream, she saw all that had just been. She saw herself coming into McCoy's house. She saw the glassed-in porch and the blue-green beauty of the mountains beyond.

She saw him open the window, and saw herself lift her face to the breeze.

And then she realized that the reality that had just passed had been her dream before. She had known that McCoy was her dream lover...

And now the lovemaking in the dream had come to pass...

Darkness seemed suddenly to descend, and with it a sense of absolute and acute terror.

Yes, the time had come.

He was out there.

The kidnapper. The murderer.

He was staring at the house. Staring, as if he could see her. As if he watched her, with McCoy.

As if he knew...

Julie awoke abruptly, a scream tearing from her lips.

He could be out there. Anywhere. Close. He could be lurking in the darkness. He could be any one of the shadows.

"Julie!"

She didn't hear McCoy call her name. She screamed again, shaking furiously, blinded by the darkness, by her fear.

"Julie!" He called her name again, pulling her into his arms, shaking her.

She didn't recognize him, McCoy thought at first. She stared straight at him, but she didn't see him. He shook her again, gently, then more fiercely. "Julie—"

"He's out there!" she cried.

"Julie, you were dreaming."

"No, no!" She fought his hold, trying to pull away from him. "You don't understand. He's out there! He's watching us, he knows us!"

"Julie, it's all right—"

"You don't believe me!" she cried frantically.

What was he supposed to believe? McCoy wondered. Her eyes were frantic. Wide, gleaming, beautiful—but frantic. He couldn't doubt the fear within them. Nor the quivering that tore at her body.

"Julie, Julie, it's all right. I'm with you." He pulled her into his arms. She was still trembling. No, shaking. Hard. He rocked with her.

A sharp unease snaked its way up his spine. She believed. No matter what, he knew that she believed. And try as he might to deny her, the creeping feeling sinking into his system seemed to say that what she told him was true.

She did know things. Julie Hatfield knew things. She had seen the black snake...

No, God! I do not believe in psychics! I believed once, I was willing to hope and pray and believe, and look what happened! I will not believe. I will never believe again.

But I love her, he thought.

And once I said I would never love again...

"He's there!" she cried more softly, her face buried against him. "The man with the scar on his shoulder."

McCoy was suddenly convinced that they were being watched.

She moaned softly. He sifted his fingers through the beautiful, tousled silkiness of her hair. It was like spun gold in the night.

"Julie, I'm with you. I won't let anything happen to you," he promised her.

She was silent. He kissed her forehead, then he rose. She started as he released her, swallowing hard, afraid for him to leave her in the darkness.

"It's all right!" he promised.

His cutoffs had dried and he slipped them on, then found the light switch. Bright light dazzled throughout the porch.

"The light!" Julie cried.

"Julie, no one can see in this room—not unless they are hovering outside in a helicopter. Look, sweetheart, you can see for yourself."

She had pulled the comforter to her chest. Wide-eyed, incredibly feminine and vulnerable with her pool of pale hair a fascinating mane around her, she turned as he directed her. And she knew that he was right. The porch did jut out to the edge of the mountain. It was a totally private retreat.

No one could see in.

But still...

"McCoy," she said softly, moistening her lips with her tongue, "he was out there. He was close. Watching. I know that he was watching the house."

He didn't say anything, but looked at his toes for a moment.

"How about that Irish coffee now? It's decaf, so we won't be up the rest of the night because of it. And we're not driving anywhere for awhile, so I can pile it high with Irish whiskey."

She almost smiled. "And add that whipped stuff, too."

He walked across the room to a closet and found her one of his terry robes. He tossed it to her. "The fit might be a bit large, but it will do in a pinch."

She slipped it on. The fit was huge, but she seemed warm and happier.

In the kitchen, they heated the coffee. Julie poured the coffee into cups, and McCoy added the whiskey.

As he had promised, he was generous. He was certain, though, that she was going to need help going back to sleep.

But even as they worked in the kitchen, he could see that she was beginning to relax again. He suggested raisin toast, and she agreed, glad to be doing something.

Their food all prepared, he suggested they take it to the porch. She tensed for a moment, then nodded and followed him as he carried the coffee and toast on a tray to the porch.

"Maybe there's a good movie on cable," he said, setting down the food tray and reaching for the remote control.

He sat cross-legged beside her before turning on the TV and cable box and flicking through the channels.

"You're going awfully fast!" she said with a laugh. "How are you going to know if you find something you want to see?"

"Oh, I always know what I want right away," he told her.

She smiled. He didn't try to pretend anymore. He took her into his arms.

"Are you okay now?"

She nodded. Then she hesitated. "He's gone."

"What?"

Her lower lip trembled just a little. "He's gone now. He was here, but he's gone now."

The feeling of unease went snaking through McCoy again.

Damned if he didn't believe her...

No. She couldn't really know things like that.

But Julie did.

Where others had failed...

He didn't want to think about it. He picked up his coffee cup with the whipped cream piled high. He touched it to hers. "Julie, I'm here. I'm with you."

"I know," she said. She leaned against him. He hadn't found a movie he wanted to see, so they watched an *I Love Lucy* rerun, an exceptionally funny one.

When they had finished the coffee and the toast, she crawled sweetly into his arms, and he made love to her again.

Afterward, he held her, smoothing her hair while she slept. No dreams marred her sleep again.

But hell, the night was shot for him.

With a sigh, he sat up and watched her. After awhile, he lay down and simply held her.

It was a long night.

In the morning, he drove her to her house before reporting in to the office.

He sat at Patty's desk, his head held morosely between his hands.

He had no leads. No damned leads at all.

"McCoy!"

He looked up. Patty gave him a friendly freckle-faced smile from over by Joe Silver's desk. She held Joe's phone receiver in her hands.

"Yeah?"

"A call for you."

"Who is it?"

"I don't know."

McCoy pushed the blinking button on the phone and picked up the receiver.

"McCoy here."

"Is that you, McCoy?"

The voice was a raspy one. Faint, almost like a whisper. It sent chills up his spine, just like nails against a blackboard.

"I just said my name." He was careful to be irritable and slow.

"She's a real looker, McCoy."

"Who are you, and what are you talking about?"

"You took her home with you last night, McCoy. And she stayed. All night."

The chills turned brutally icy. They stole his breath while fear and fury streaked through him.

"Who the hell are you—"

"Oh, no. I can't tell you that."

McCoy motioned wildly to Patty to get a trace going on the call. "Well, what can you tell me at the moment?"

Soft, husky, rasping laughter came his way. His fingers tightened around the receiver.

"You're not going to trace me, McCoy. We'll talk later."

"Wait! When? I don't know who—"

"Ah, but I know who you are. You kept my money, McCoy. Yes, I know you well. And I know her."

"What the hell—"

The phone clicked dead.

He stared across the room at Patty. She shook her head sadly.

Not enough time for a trace.

She had known! Julie had known!

Someone had been watching them on that mountaintop!

Chapter 8

It was strange, but by the morning, Julie didn't find herself plagued at all by the fear that had come to her in the night.

She knew she had lived out her dream, and she and McCoy had made it through the night.

McCoy wasn't part of the danger—he was her only protection from the danger, she was certain of it. The danger came from the kidnapper, the man with the scar on his shoulder, the man who had taken Tracy Nicholson and the other two young women.

And maybe the man had been somewhere near them last night. He was certainly still in the vicinity. That was why she was so certain that she was being watched.

McCoy had been wonderful last night. He hadn't ridiculed her. But then, she had been so terrified, and he had known it.

By morning, though, he had been very quiet. Pensive. She couldn't tell if he had decided she was neurotic or that there might be something to her perceptions. He was too hard-nosed to give her a clue. And he had let her off with the usual stern warnings. Don't open the doors. Be careful. Be really careful. Use the peephole, and the latches.

After he had brought her home, she convinced herself that she was going to tackle her office—clean out all the paperwork and pay her bills before someone came after her—and then vacuum, dust, rearrange, the whole nine yards. She wanted to call Brenda Maitland; she was certain that Brenda wouldn't mind telling her all sorts of things about McCoy that Julie wanted to know.

Julie didn't want to call Brenda too early just in case she slept late, but then, halfway through what she liked to think of creative money management—making sure that she paid the bills that politely reminded her that she was late—she realized that Brenda Maitland couldn't possibly sleep late, she had two children to get off to school.

She pored through the phone books, looking for Brenda Maitland. She couldn't find the name, so she called information, only to discover that Brenda's number was unlisted. She almost called the station to see if McCoy was there and ask him for his sister's phone number, but then, she didn't want him to know that she meant to give Brenda the third degree on him.

Perplexed, Julie sat on the porch, looking out over her own mountain, wishing she had the power to foretell the future at will, and wondering if she and McCoy would ever manage to really get along.

"Right. I knew that. But I wanted to give you fair warning just in case...oh, never mind. Now, of course, you want to know just what his problem is with you, right?"

Julie inhaled quickly, then laughed. "Well, yes, in a nutshell, that's it."

"He doesn't believe in psychics," Brenda said softly.

"Yes, he's made that very clear. I can't even mention anything about it, or he's down my throat."

"He doesn't mean to be," Brenda said. She smoothed a strand of hair, biting softly on her lower lip. "There's the restaurant. Let's wait till we get inside, shall we?"

"Yes, fine," Julie said. But it wasn't fine. Her curiosity was driving her crazy, but what Brenda had to tell her seemed to be something very important.

The restaurant was pretty and bright, with broad picture windows and lots of ferns. They were led to a table by one of the big windows. The hostess chatted until the waitress brought the menus.

Then the waitress chatted, pointing out the different specialties, making suggestions. Julie kept smiling politely, wishing with all her heart that the waitress would go away.

"What do you think? Cajun chicken salad and gumbo sounds intriguing."

"It sounds just great," Julie said. Anything sounded great, just so long as the waitress would disappear.

"I don't know. I'm still wavering between that and the Hawaiian Caesar," Brenda murmured. "Or then there's the taco salad—that looks great, too."

"Oh, the taco is super!" the waitress said.

"Let's make it tacos, then," Julie said enthusiastically.

To her relief, Julie saw that she had won Brenda over. They both ordered iced tea, too, and then the young woman left them. Julie leaned forward, waiting expectantly.

"Okay, Brenda, please! Explain to me your brother's big problem with psychics!"

"Well, you see, he was married," Brenda began.

"Married!" Julie murmured.

"She was beautiful, really sweet. Serena was a Californian. He met her at George Washington University. They were really perfect for one another."

Julie shook her head. "Brenda, what would your brother's marital status have to do with psychics? Oh! Did they have problems because of an astrology reading or something?"

"Oh, no!" Brenda exclaimed. Then she fell silent, smiling. Their iced tea had arrived.

The waitress left them once again.

"Oh, Julie, if only it were something that simple!"

"Then..."

"You really do care a lot about him, don't you?" Brenda asked her.

"I—yes," Julie admitted flatly.

"Umm. And you're sleeping with him, huh?"

"Brenda, I—"

"Never mind, don't answer that. It's none of my business, and it was an awful question." But she smiled. "Especially when I know the answer."

"Brenda!" Julie moaned. "Will you please tell me what happened with the psychic?"

"I am sorry. Well, it had to do with his work," she began, then she broke off abruptly, frowning. "I don't believe it!" she said, looking over Julie's shoulder through the glass window and out to the parking lot.

"What?" Julie demanded. She swung around. To her amazement, she saw McCoy's big Lincoln parked next to his sister's BMW.

And McCoy was coming through the door.

He stopped as the hostess addressed him, but Julie saw him pointing toward her and Brenda. She couldn't begin to read his thoughts because it was another black-leather-jacket-and-dark-sunglasses day. He seemed casual enough, clad in jeans, his hands in his pockets. But Julie sensed a tension about him that hadn't been there before.

Certainly not last night. When she had been so unreasonably frightened, he had been like a rock. He hadn't ridiculed her, but she had been certain that he hadn't put any credence in her belief that they were being watched.

What was he doing here? she wondered. Was he looking for her, or for Brenda?

And why had he shown up just when she had discovered that he'd had a wife, and that something had happened to her?

Something that had had to do with a psychic.

"Robert!" Brenda said, her voice echoing the amazement Julie was feeling that he could have stumbled upon them.

Had he sensed that she planned to talk to his sister, trying to delve into his life?

Perhaps. His tension seemed like anger when he reached the table and sat beside Julie. He scarcely gave her a chance to move over. With him next to her, she felt his tension more keenly.

"Things slow down at the station?" Brenda asked, trying for a smile. Maybe she was feeling a bit guilty, too. As if he might have known that she was waiting to spill the beans about him.

"No, things were not slow at the station," he replied, scowling. "I was looking for Julie."

"Why?" Julie asked, surprised.

"Because I've got something for you."

"Really?" Julie said. He had something for her. He had that look that he had worn when they had first collided. It was not a look she expected to see on the face of a man who wanted to give her a present. "What is it?"

"It's in the car," he began.

"How did you find us?" Brenda demanded.

Intuition, Julie thought suddenly. Simple intuition. He denies it, but he has a certain power all his own.

"Easy. She wasn't home—I couldn't find you at home or at your office. And I know that women love to gossip."

Brenda wrinkled her nose at him. "Julie is going to think you're incredibly rude."

"Julie knows he's incredibly rude," Julie said.

She felt the sharpness of his silver gaze, right through the darkness of his glasses. "You should keep that in mind, Miss Hatfield," he murmured.

She didn't have a chance to wonder what he meant, for the waitress was back with their salads. McCoy looked at the giant shells piled high with lettuce and ground beef, olives, salsa and sour cream.

"What is it?"

"Something green," Brenda said. "I don't think you'd care for it. They do have hamburgers."

McCoy shook his head and waved over the waitress. "I'm not hungry—but I'll have a cup of coffee," he told the young woman.

"How did you find us?" Brenda persisted.

McCoy sighed. "I figured you might be together."

"Almost as if you had second sight," Julie murmured innocently.

He made a not very delicate snorting sound. "Once I knew you were together, it was easy. I just needed to think of a place where the food was all green. And I knew this place was here, near Brenda's, and new. It has nothing to do with second sight. It has everything to do with logical thinking," he said. His tone was almost fierce.

Julie stared at him, startled by his tone, wondering what had happened to cause the change in him since he had left her that morning.

"Well, you're a great lunch companion," Brenda said, attacking her salad. "If I'd had any idea you were going to be so charming, I would have called and invited you."

He drummed his fingers on the table, eyeing his sister. "Why? Am I disturbing you?"

Yes! Julie wanted to shout. She had just been on the verge of finding something out. And now...

"Why did you have to hunt us down?" Brenda demanded.

"I told you—I have something for Julie."

"Well, couldn't it wait?" Brenda demanded, exasperated.

He shook his head. "No, Brenda, it couldn't wait. It's not even going to make it through that salad if you don't hurry up!"

The waitress brought McCoy his coffee.

"I'm chewing, I'm chewing," Brenda said.

McCoy looked into Julie's bowl. "That's red meat in there," he warned her.

"I do eat red meat, McCoy," she reminded him.

It didn't matter. Since he had arrived, Julie had lost her appetite. Her nerves felt all twisted into knots. He was angry, he was tense. She didn't think that his anger should have been directed toward her, but somehow she was receiving the brunt of it.

And he had something for her...

Brenda's mind was moving in the same direction. "Isn't it wonderful to receive gifts from nice, handsome, charming men?" she commented sweetly.

"Eat, Brenda," McCoy said.

"I know!" Brenda exclaimed. "It's a diamond!"

They both glared at her. Brenda chuckled softly. "Well, is it intimate? Should I slink out and leave in my own car?"

"Brenda, you should finish your lunch," McCoy said flatly.

Julie could see the steam issuing from his coffee, but he managed to gulp it down anyway. He noticed that Julie was finished with her lunch, and he turned his attention to Brenda.

"Aren't you done yet?"

"Well, yes, I suppose, if you want me to be!" Brenda exclaimed.

"You know, McCoy, this better be good," Julie warned him, her eyes narrowing at his impatience with his sister.

"It just can't wait in the car any longer," McCoy said. "Come on."

"Gee, let's remember not to invite him to lunch anymore, shall we?" Julie said to Brenda.

"Never," Brenda agreed solemnly.

"Would you just—"

"We have to pay the check!" Julie said. "They frown on people who eat and leave without paying. They might even call in the police!"

Brenda said she'd leave a tip, and Julie pushed past McCoy, catching their waitress by the cash register. When she turned, McCoy was waiting at the door. He was holding it open for her.

Julie watched him as she walked out the door, wondering how someone could seem so furious with her and be so determined to give her a gift.

"Will you please hurry?" he demanded.

"I'm here now!" she exclaimed. "But what can make you so impatient I can't begin to—"

She broke off because she suddenly saw why he hadn't wanted to stay in the restaurant.

His gift, waiting in the Lincoln, was panting.

Just as she came outside, the creature stuck its huge head out of the window.

She'd never seen such a large head on a dog, nor had she ever seen a dog quite like this one. For a moment she wondered if it was beautiful—or the ugliest dog she had ever come across.

It was certainly the biggest.

"You're giving her a monster?" Brenda demanded incredulously.

"He's not a monster," McCoy said indignantly. "He's half shepherd and half Rottweiler."

Julie stared blankly at McCoy. Of all the things she might have expected, it was certainly not a dog big enough to eat her out of house and home.

She searched her mind frantically. Had she ever given him the slightest reason to think that she had wanted a dog? No...she was certain that she hadn't. And if someone had asked her to please think about what kind of dog she'd like, she'd have probably said that her favorite might be a beagle or a Scottie, or something fairly small—and cute.

This dog could never, never be described as cute.

"You'll get to like him," McCoy assured her. He walked to his car and opened the back door. The creature hopped out. His head came nearly to McCoy's hip.

"He's bigger than Julie is," Brenda stated. Brenda seemed convinced that her brother had lost his mind. "Actually, Robert, it might have been a bit premature, but personally, I think that the diamond would have been a better idea."

McCoy ignored her. "His name is Rusty," he told Julie.

"Rusty. Nice name," Julie murmured. She stared at Rusty. He cocked his head at her, as if he knew he was being judged. A massive, shepherdlike tail began to wag, and Rusty gave a little whine.

He had great eyes, Julie decided at last. Big, brown, mournful eyes. He looked at her as if he knew that she was supposed to be his master, as if he knew it was necessary for her to like him.

"Rusty, Julie," McCoy said. The dog trotted forward a few steps to Julie. He pressed a cold nose against her hand.

"Hi, Rusty," Julie said.

"Robert, this is a restaurant parking lot," Brenda reminded him. "We're going to scare away all the clientele with that monster."

"He's not a monster."

"He's ugly as hell!"

"He was the best in his class," McCoy retorted.

Julie stared at him again, her eyes narrowing. "Maybe we should head back to Brenda's," she murmured.

"Rusty's not getting in my car!" Brenda said with a laugh.

"No, he's not, he's getting in mine," McCoy told her. "And don't you ever beg me for a fine dog like Rusty, little sister, because after this, you'll never get one from me!"

"Thank God!" Brenda said, laughing. "Julie, you go ahead with that new creature of yours. Or both those creatures of yours. I'm going for my kids. I'll meet you at my house." Brenda waved and started for her car.

"Come on, Rusty, let's go," McCoy told the dog.

As obediently as if he understood every inflection of every word, Rusty turned and hopped into the backseat. Julie walked around to sit next to McCoy in the front passenger seat.

As they headed out of the parking lot, she exploded with a, "But why?"

He hesitated, as if he didn't want to answer her. Then he smiled. "Didn't you always want a big old dog?"

"No, not really," she admitted, but she had to smile. He was trying. She'd give him that.

"How about a thank-you gift?" he said huskily.

"Flowers would have done fine," she said.

He was silent for just a second. "Julie, the kidnapper called me today."

"What?" she gasped, turning to him. Despite his dark glasses, she could see the gravity in his features. She bit her lower lip.

The kidnapper had called him. Was that the danger she had seen in the dream that had become reality now?

"What—what did he say? How did you know it was him?"

McCoy shrugged. She wondered if he was hedging. "He didn't say too much of anything. I knew it was him because I'll never forget his voice. Julie, he knows me. He knows what is going on around me. I'll just feel better if you're not alone."

She looked at her hands. They were shaking. She clenched them, determined that he wouldn't see she had suddenly felt a terrible sweep of fear come rushing over her.

"McCoy, I keep a gun. It's a little ladies' Colt. Petty taught me how to use it. I'm actually pretty good at a firing range."

He turned to her, a wry smile twisting his lips. "Is poor Rusty really that ugly? I thought he was a great-looking dog. I spent hours with the trainer before making my final choice. He was on special request for a cop in the D.C. area, but I convinced the guy I needed him more. He's perfectly housebroken. And he'll obey every command you give him."

"A dog is better than a gun?" Julie said.

"A dog senses things when you're asleep. Can a gun do that?"

Julie laughed softly. "I guess not." She was suddenly touched. McCoy had taken a lot of effort to get the dog for her. He had probably done some heavy-duty bargaining. And a dog like Rusty had probably been a very expensive investment, too.

Maybe more than a diamond—a small diamond, anyway.

She turned to look at Rusty. His face was a perfect cross between Rottweiller and shepherd, with shepherdesque markings. Those huge brown eyes looked at her soulfully. He wagged his massive tail, and barked once.

"He's . . . he's great," Julie said.

She saw McCoy smile, and was convinced that he thought she was merely humoring him. It didn't seem to matter.

Just so long as she kept the dog.

Julie sat back as he drove. "It's very strange, you know."

"What's so strange?"

"Well, you don't seem to have any problems thinking that a dog can have a sixth sense."

She watched as his fingers tightened around the wheel. "I never said that a dog had a sixth sense. A dog has an excellent sense of smell and very acute hearing. And this fellow should scare away almost anyone."

Julie couldn't argue with that.

They pulled into Brenda's driveway well ahead of Brenda. McCoy said that she needed to get to know Rusty. And although Rusty might be one of the most obedient dogs in the world, McCoy seemed determined to teach her how to give instructions. So out in front of Brenda's farmhouse they worked with Rusty. Julie told him to come, to heel, to lie down and to play dead. She told him to bark, and she told him to be quiet.

"Is that it?" Julie asked McCoy.

"Not quite," McCoy said grimly.

"Well?"

"You can tell him to attack," McCoy said very softly. "Just remember that if you do, he'll take hold of the person by the throat and throw the full force of his weight upon him."

"Will he..."

"No, he won't rip the throat out, he'll just stay there, forever if need be, until he's told to get off. I watched him working with the dummy. If a fool tried to fight him, the fool could be pretty well ripped up."

Julie turned away uneasily.

McCoy spun her around. "Julie, this man has tried to kill three times. We can only assume that he succeeded once, since only one young woman has never been found. He tried to kill a child, Julie."

She nodded. "Yes, I know."

Brenda's car pulled up the drive. She had barely braked it to a halt before Taylor and Tammy leaped out and ran to McCoy. "Uncle Robert, Mom's been telling us about the dog for Julie!" Taylor called out. Then he saw the dog. "Oh, wow, he's great!"

"He's not as ugly as all sin, Mom," Tammy cried, puzzled as she studied poor Rusty.

"Well, maybe he's only as ugly as half of all sin!" Brenda called out cheerfully. Then she became somber as she stepped out of the car. "Robert, Rusty won't hurt the kids, will he?"

"Definitely not," McCoy said. And it was a good thing, of course, because the kids were already on the ground with Rusty, shrieking with laughter as they rolled over and over with the giant canine. Brenda, coming up to stand between McCoy and Julie, gave her grudging approval at last.

"Well, he is quite a creature, isn't he?" she said. "Julie, before you leave, I thought of a few things my brother didn't. I have some bowls and a twenty-five-pound bag of dog chow in my trunk. That'll last you until at least tomorrow."

Julie smiled. "Thanks."

"And since my brother decided not to let anyone enjoy lunch, I picked up some burgers to barbecue."

"Brenda, I have to go back to the station," McCoy began.

"Oh, you have another hour, I'm sure."

"They're turkey burgers, Uncle Robert," Tammy said.

McCoy groaned. "I don't think I have an hour—"

"You weren't supposed to tell him!" Brenda moaned.

"Honest, Uncle Robert," Taylor advised him, one man to another. "You really can't tell the difference. They're pretty good. I eat them."

"Oh, well. If my nephew eats them, they can't be all bad. But really, Brenda, I've got to go back to work. Hurry it up, will you?"

"Yes, sir!"

"I'll give you a hand," Julie said.

"No, no. You get to know your creature. There really isn't anything to do. The barbecue is all set, I have those quick-burning coals. And I have store-bought tossed salad, macaroni salad and chips. It will only take a few minutes."

She smiled merrily and went off, Tammy following behind her like a very mature little helper.

"He really is a great dog, Uncle Robert," Taylor said.

"Yeah? You think so?" McCoy said, ruffling his nephew's hair.

"You can come see him anytime you want," Julie said. "And if your mom is real busy, I can bring him here sometimes."

McCoy knelt by Taylor and threw a stick. Rusty began to bark and bellow, then chased after it. "Guess what, Taylor."

"What?"

"Rusty has a brother. But don't tell your mom yet. I want her to suffer."

"Uncle Robert, I'll be the one suffering!" Taylor said.

McCoy laughed. "Well, we'll see. I'm going to have to break this to her gently." He glared at Julie. "Don't you say anything to her, either."

"Not a word!" Julie said.

Brenda poked her head out the door. "Come on in. Taylor, you can give that monster some water and a bowl of dog food. Julie, Robert, you can wash up and grab the plates—it's paper and plastic tonight, all right?"

"Sounds great!" Julie said.

"Taylor, get the hose out in back for his water, huh?"

"Yes, ma'am." Taylor went off as he was told. McCoy and Brenda watched as Julie knelt and patted Rusty on the head. He rewarded her with a lick of the tongue that seemed to encompass her entire face. "Yuck!" She laughed. "Brenda, I think I need a bath!" she wailed.

"Oh, quit being such a fuss!" McCoy said flatly.

She stood indignantly. "Well, excuse me. You just remember that if he decides to sleep in bed with me. My room is small," she warned McCoy softly.

"What was that?" Brenda asked. She had heard. That soft blue glitter of mischief was in her eyes.

Julie flushed and McCoy laughed. "Do you ladies have to tell each other everything?" he whispered.

She let out a sigh of exasperation and spun around, heading for the house. "He deserves turkey burgers nightly!" she told Brenda.

Actually, the turkey burgers were very good, and piled high with lettuce and tomatoes and pickles, they resembled their beef cousins to a T. McCoy commented to his sister that they were delicious.

They ate at the picnic table in the backyard. The children sat for at least ten minutes, dutifully eating one burger each, making their mother happy by quickly consuming salad, then jumped up to play with the dog.

Rusty hadn't stayed around the table. Julie hadn't had the heart to send him away when he had come sniffing, but McCoy had ordered him to go sit, and that was exactly what the dog had done.

But when the kids rose to go play with him, McCoy let them each take half a turkey burger to give to Rusty. The kids, delighted, fed him.

And Rusty, delighted, lapped up the turkey burger.

Then the three of them raced around the big lawn. The kids shrieked with gales of laughter. Rusty barked now and then, his furry tail flying.

"I think I'm going to feel guilty taking him home," Julie said.

"Oh, no, no, no!" Brenda laughed. "The housing market hasn't been that good lately. I sprung for the puppy chow today. Now it's in your lap."

McCoy took a long swig of soda. "Every boy should have a dog," he said. "And that Taylor, he's a good kid."

"Didn't you say that you had to go back to work, Robert?" Brenda asked him.

He laughed. "Yeah, I do. Come on, Julie. I'll follow you home."

She looked up, startled.

"Julie doesn't have to go to work, you do."

"I'm going to follow her home," McCoy said simply. He stood and kissed his sister on top of the head. "Thanks for dinner. It was great. Julie, come on."

"Has he always had this illusion that he's a drill sergeant?" Julie asked Brenda. She wasn't going, she decided.

"It only comes out at times," Brenda promised her.

"Julie!" He turned to look across the yard where the kids were playing with Rusty. "Hey, Rusty, come!"

Rusty barked and came bounding toward him. "See? Look how good Rusty is—no complaints," McCoy told Julie.

"That's right, McCoy. Something you should bear in mind. Rusty is obedient, and I am not," Julie said with feigned patience. "Rusty is a dog, and I am a woman."

McCoy laughed. "All right. Come here, woman. Let's go. Please!"

All right. It was the "please" that did it. She'd go. She didn't know why he was so determined to follow her home, but he was.

She thanked Brenda for dinner and was pleasantly touched when both kids—manly Taylor included—offered her a kiss on the cheek goodbye. Then she was packed into her car, and McCoy was behind her with Rusty in his backseat, his big head sticking out the window.

"You should be the one to keep that dog, McCoy!" she said softly beneath her breath.

She pulled up to her own mountain. McCoy came behind her just as she was dragging Brenda's gift of the twenty-five pounds of dog food out of the car. "I'll get it," McCoy told her. He carried the food into her kitchen, Rusty following behind him, his tail wagging.

"There are rules here," Julie warned the dog. "The kitchen is yours, the porch is yours. Upstairs is a no-no. I will not have fleas where I sleep."

"Are you insinuating that I would buy you a dog with fleas?" McCoy inquired. "Or are you just trying to keep him out of my half of the bed?"

She had to laugh at the inquiry. Then she realized that his eyes were on fire, that a slow grin was sensually curling his lip. He took a step toward her.

"McCoy, you said you have to go back to work," she reminded him.

"I do," he told her. But he was closer. And she was suddenly in his arms. And his kiss had the same sizzling appeal it had always had.

Yes, he had to go back to work. But apparently, he had a little time. Before she knew it, they were upstairs. And their clothing seemed to be melting away.

And the world disappeared as he made love to her.

Yet, as he lay beside her later, his chest glistening in the moonlight that flickered into her room, he seemed more distant than ever before. He rose, walked to the window, then came back to her.

"I have to go."

"Are you coming back tonight?" she asked.

He hesitated. "No. I'll be busy."

She gritted her teeth. He wasn't going to be busy. And he wasn't coming back tomorrow, or the day after. She knew it. What she didn't know was why.

"Fine."

"Julie—"

"Never mind! Just go."

"Damn you, Julie, if you just understood—"

"Well, I don't, because you never want to tell me anything. And you're making me neurotic. One minute you can't leave my side, and the next minute you're climbing out of bed to tell me that you don't want to see me again."

"I didn't say that—"

"I'm a psychic, remember?" she said curtly. He wasn't coming back, she thought with panic. At least, that was what he was thinking at the moment.

And everything still seemed so intimate between them. They were both naked, slick, warm. They should have been content. They should have been curled into one another's arms.

She leaped up, wrenched her robe from the foot of her bed and slipped into it. She tied the belt in a knot as she continued speaking to him.

"But then, that is the problem, isn't it? You'd be perfectly happy if I'd just pretend that none of it existed. Well, I can't!"

"Julie, damn you!"

He was sputtering. She was right. But suddenly he jerked her into his arms.

And kissed her again.

And it was all there. All the passion, all the demand. All the hunger.

Maybe even love...

But then he broke from her abruptly. "I have to go."

She stepped back, tears stinging her eyes as he dressed.

"Julie—"

"You said that you had to go," she said flatly.

He didn't try to argue with her. He left her in the room. She heard his footsteps as he hurried down the hallway—and then the door slammed.

Then she heard his bellow far beneath her. "Come lock this door!"

"I have a monster of a dog," she muttered to herself. "Why do I have to lock the damned door?"

But she went downstairs and did so. She leaned against the door while she heard him gun his motor, then drive away.

"I hate him!" she said out loud. Then she added softly, "I think I love him. I really do."

Rusty came and stuck his cold wet nose into her hand while he wagged his tail, waiting to be petted. Absently, Julie obliged him.

"What makes him tick, Rusty?" she said to the dog. "He can't seem to stay away, he buys me presents—like you. And then..."

She paused, realizing that she still didn't really know what Brenda had been about to tell her about her brother.

He had been married. That was all she knew.

"So what happened to his wife, Rusty? And why did it make him hate psychics?"

Rusty barked.

"I swear, I am going to find out tomorrow!" Julie vowed.

But the questions seemed to plague her relentlessly.

It was going to be a long, long night.

Chapter 9

By the next evening, Julie was frustrated. She hadn't heard from McCoy.

And she hadn't been able to reach Brenda, either. She had tried the business number through most of the day, but had managed to speak with nothing but Brenda's answering machine.

She had tried to concentrate on a new story, but had quickly given up the effort. Then she had tried to read a new mystery that she had been dying to sink her teeth into, but she couldn't concentrate on any printed matter any more completely than she could concentrate on her own.

At six she sat on her front steps, idly patting Rusty, who had worn himself out running around, and now sat contented by her side, half of his big body on one step, half of it on another.

Suddenly, Rusty sat up and started to bark.

"What is it?" Julie asked the dog. Then she saw. One of Petty's police patrol cars was winding its way up her little patch of mountain.

"Who is it, huh?" She felt herself tighten from head to toe, hoping that it was going to be McCoy. She knew, though, that he wouldn't be in the cruiser. And when the car pulled to a halt in front of her house, she quickly saw that Patty was driving and Joe Silver was at her side.

The two exited the car smiling. Then Rusty started to bark and bellow.

The smile quickly left Patty's pretty freckled face and she stopped dead still. Joe's brown gaze became somber, and he, too, stopped walking.

"It's all right!" Julie called quickly. She put a firm hand on Rusty's collar. "Rusty, these are the cops!" she remonstrated to the dog. "He's supposed to be so damned well trained!" she called out. "A burglar will come and good old Rusty will probably lead him to the silver! Rusty, they're friends. Sit!"

Rusty whined but immediately dropped at her feet. He put his nose between his paws.

"Where on earth did he come from?" Patty asked her.

"You didn't know anything about him?" Julie said.

Joe walked up, smiling again. "I didn't know anything, but I imagine that I can guess. McCoy bought him for you, right?"

Julie glanced at Joe and shrugged. "Yes, McCoy gave him to me."

"The guy doesn't believe in flowers or candy, huh?" Patty said, still studying the dog. She gazed at Julie again. "Is he hideous or beautiful? I'll be damned if I can tell."

Joe laughed. "Shepherd and Rottweiler, I think. Look at that head! What does he eat?"

"Anything and everything, so it seems," Julie said with a sigh. He was a great dog, really. He was housebroken, and he did have the biggest, most soulful brown eyes she had ever seen in that huge head of his.

But last night he hadn't liked being kept downstairs while Julie slept. He'd found one of her old slippers and chewed it into pulp.

"What's his name?" Joe asked.

"Rusty."

"Hello, Rusty," Patty said.

Rusty growled.

"Never mind, Rusty."

"There's nothing wrong, is there?" Julie asked, looking from one to the other. "Did Petty send for me for some reason or another? You know, he can just call. He doesn't need to send you two out all of the time."

"Petty didn't send us at all," Patty told her.

"McCoy asked us to come out."

"McCoy!" Julie said, startled. But then it all made sense. He wasn't coming around himself. He was going to do his best to distance himself from her.

He was worried about her, though. So he'd given her a dog, and now he was sending out his troops.

Patty shrugged. "I told him that I'd call you, but he wanted us to come out and take a look around. Who knows, maybe he wants *someone* to see that police cruisers can be at your house [illegible] quickly."

"Maybe," Julie murmured. She gritted her teeth, wondering why it hurt so badly that McCoy suddenly seemed so determined to shake her off. She should be furious. He was absolutely incredible. He came on like a cyclone. He seemed to be following her wherever she went, and he had appeared at the lunch table when she had least wanted him to do so.

And then her house...

The sweet tension had been there. The electric need. And he had seemed to want her so damned badly...

But as soon as that tempest had ended, he had withdrawn. Completely.

"Well," she said brightly, determined not to let anyone see that she could be affected by Robert McCoy in any way, shape, or form. "What are you two up to now?" She gazed at her watch. "It's past six. Want to come in for a while?"

"I'm not so sure that we can," Joe said, laughing. He pointed at Rusty, who had lodged his bulk in front of Julie's door.

"Rusty!" Julie moaned. "Give me a second. I'll put him in the basement."

Rusty whined and cast all his weight on his haunches, but Julie was determined. She dragged the huge dog through the front door, the entryway, and into the kitchen. She panted as she held him by the collar and opened the basement door. "I'm sorry, Rusty, but you just can't be nasty to my friends like that!"

When she turned around, Joe and Patty had followed her into the kitchen. Patty was in the refrigerator. "What have you got that's cold?"

"Are you off duty?" Julie asked.

"Yep. You were our last official project. You're fine. At least, she looks fine to me," Patty said.

"Looks great to me," Joe agreed. "Have you got any cold beer in there?"

Julie stepped around Patty and found a can of beer and tossed it over to Joe. "White Zinfandel, white Zinfandel," Patty murmured.

"Boy, she's even specific," Julie moaned to Joe.

"Hey, Patty, beggars are not supposed to be choosers," Joe reprimanded her.

"But I know she's got it in here somewhere—beyond all the green stuff," Patty teased.

"Move!" Julie commanded. She found the wine and poured a glass for Patty, then sat on one of the bar stools at the kitchen counter. "How are things going?" she asked.

Joe shrugged. "There was a break-in at Mike Geary's souvenir store," he said.

She shook her head. "I'm talking about the kidnapping. Or kidnappings. Any news?"

Joe shook his head. "Not that I know of."

"Something happened yesterday."

"What?" Julie demanded.

"Yeah, what?" Joe echoed.

Patty stared at him incredulously. "You didn't hear? Oh, I can't believe I forgot to tell you. I was alone in the office with McCoy when somebody called and asked to speak with him. I didn't think anything of it at first. Then all of a sudden McCoy is waving at me madly, indicating that I should get a trace going on the call. I tried, but I'd barely gotten things started before the caller hung up."

"The kidnapper?" Julie said.

"I imagine. Or else somebody claiming to be the kidnapper."

"What did he say?" Julie asked.

"I didn't get a chance to hear—"

"Well, what did McCoy say?"

"McCoy didn't say anything, not to me. He was closeted with Petty this morning for awhile, so I guess the two of them really hashed it out. Whatever he said, though, it disturbed the hell out of McCoy."

Julie stared at Joe. He shrugged helplessly. "This is the first that I'm hearing about it, too."

"Well, they must be trying to keep a really low profile," Julie mused. "But—how could he be sure it was the kidnapper?"

"I think," Patty told her, pulling up a bar stool, "that McCoy had no doubt. Don't forget, Julie, McCoy listened to the kidnapper's voice time and time again on the night you two went from phone booth to phone booth trying to find Tracy Nicholson."

"I had forgotten," Julie said thoughtfully. She shrugged. "I don't know. Maybe he's just trying to make sure that he doesn't say anything to the two of you, or to Timothy, or even Petty—anyone who might say something to me. He's probably afraid that I hear things and then imagine that they're part of my abilities."

"Oh, don't take it that way!" Patty said.

"And why not?"

Patty paused, blinked, then shrugged. "He must think a great deal of you."

"He must," Joe agreed cheerfully. He leaned on the counter, cupping his chin in his hand. "Hey, kid, that's an expensive dog he bought for you!"

"Yeah, boy," Patty agreed. "I didn't even know that you were actually dating."

"I don't think that we are actually dating," Julie said. She didn't want to discuss it any longer. She leaped off her seat. "So, Patty, are we going to see a movie, or what? I'm sorry, Joe, do you want to join us?"

"No, thanks," he said. "I've got plans."

"I think he has a very hot date, but he doesn't want to tell me about it," Patty moaned.

"Yeah. Every law-enforcement official in the next three states will be talking about my love life if I tell Patty anything," Joe said flatly.

"Oh, come now!" Patty protested.

"Timothy Riker went out with a Las Vegas showgirl last year and I swear, they knew about it in Maine," Joe told Julie. "Ladies, with that, I am leaving. Have a nice night." He paused a moment. "Hey, Julie, will you see that my partner here makes it home?"

"Of course," Julie assured him. He waved again. Patty made a face at him, and he was gone.

"What do you want to see?" Patty asked Julie. "Have you got a newspaper around here?"

Julie indicated the newspaper at the end of the counter. Patty started looking through it. "I wanted to go home and take a shower," she murmured. "But if we want to eat first—do we want to eat first?"

"Yes," Julie said. "And I want to eat somewhere with lots of alfalfa sprouts."

"Alfalfa sprouts?" Patty said.

"Never mind," Julie murmured. "How about seafood?"

"Whatever," Patty said, poring over the movie section. "Comedy? History? Drama, suspense, murder—no, no murder. How about the new thing they've been advertising—"

"Comedy?" Julie asked.

"Yeah."

"Perfect," Julie agreed. She wanted to see something she could just sit through. Her concentration probably wouldn't be the best. She glanced at her watch. "Hey, we'd probably best be getting a move on here. Although, if you want to shower here, there's probably time. You can find something of mine to wear, and we can still make dinner in plenty of time if we go to that seafood place right by the theater."

"Well, it sounds like a hunk of heaven," Patty said dryly. "All I'd need is a good-looking guy to go with it."

"They're not all that they're cracked up to be," Julie said.

"I'd like the chance to find out," Patty said with a laugh. Then her eyes twinkled with merriment as she studied Julie. "I just can't wait to get all the dirt on McCoy. Is the feud over? What do you mean, you're not dating? Just flat out sleeping together? What's he like in bed? Is he just great?"

"Patty, you are asking very personal questions," Julie moaned.

"Hey. They're the best kind. Come on. Tell all."

"Patty, you've got about five minutes to shower."

"Hell, I'll give up the shower for the information."

"Well you're not getting any information, so go get ready."

"Well, all right. But as good-looking as McCoy is, I think you need to think about this one seriously. After all, if he bought you this giant dog after just a few dates, or sessions, or whatever you're having, imagine what he'd get you for a first anniversary present? An African elephant would not be out of the question."

"Would you please go get ready!" Julie commanded. Patty laughed and went upstairs.

Julie started to lock up the house, then remembered Rusty in the basement. She opened the door, calling to him. Absently she patted him on the head and straightened the kitchen. She heard Patty ask if she could wear a certain pair of jeans and Julie called back that she could wear anything that she wanted.

Then Patty came running down the stairs, and Julie went up to brush her teeth and her hair. She grabbed a jacket and her shoulder bag and hurried down the stairs.

Patty had stepped outside and was sitting on the porch, as Julie had been when Patty and Joe had arrived. Rusty had decided to like her. He was slumped on the porch, his nose in Patty's lap. "Sorry, Rusty, we've got to go," Julie said. "I've got to put you inside."

"He seems to like the outside. Maybe you should just leave him on the porch."

"But he's supposed to protect the house. I think he needs to do that from inside."

"Maybe," Patty agreed.

Julie shooed the dog in the house, and the two of them left. She winced, hearing him bark mournfully as they drove away.

"So what is the story with McCoy?" Patty persisted, watching Julie as she drove.

"I don't think there is a story right now, and I really don't want to talk about it," Julie told her.

"Oh, come on—"

"No. I'm serious. Patty, you believe in me, even if he doesn't, right? Well, I knew when he left last night that he didn't mean to come back, that he intends to stay away. For some reason. I don't know why. And he hates psychics to begin with. For—" She broke off, ready to kick herself. She still hadn't gotten hold of Brenda.

"For?" Patty persisted.

"Nothing. I really don't know, and I really don't want to talk about it, all right?"

Patty sighed. "But—"

"Whatever was is over. All right?"

"Fine! I won't push the future! But you can tell me about the past, okay? Is he just the greatest thing since the invention of chewing gum?"

Julie groaned out loud. "Patty!"

"Okay, okay."

And Julie was certain that Patty did try, but try or not, all she did was ask questions about McCoy all through dinner.

And even during the movie, despite the fact that Patty was entertained at last, Julie couldn't get her mind off McCoy. The whole thing was so crazy.

It must have been a good movie, because everyone else in the audience kept laughing hysterically. Patty was laughing so hard that she punched Julie on occasion.

Damn McCoy. She couldn't even enjoy a movie anymore!

She stood up suddenly, determined to leave the theater and find a phone.

"Julie!" Patty said. "I've got more popcorn here—"

"I'm not going for popcorn," she whispered.

"Ladies, please?" the fat man behind them intoned.

Julie apologized, quickly slipped from her row and hurried from the movie. In the lobby, she found a phone, and dialed Brenda's number.

She had no difficulty. She had called McCoy's sister so many times now that she knew the number by heart.

"Oh, Brenda, come on, please!" she murmured. She was delighted when the phone was answered.

"Hello?"

"Brenda, it's Julie!"

"Julie! Hi, I've been trying to get you back—"

"I know. I'm not home. I'm at the movies."

"Oh. What are you seeing?"

Julie told her.

"Oh, I've been dying to see that! Is it as good as they say?"

"I guess so. The whole audience is laughing."

"Oh, my lord, but I never finished telling you the end of the story about Robert! Oh, Julie, I forgot, or I would have made sure to reach you today."

"Can you tell me now?"

"Yes, of course. Julie, he's really not as bad a bear as maybe he seems at times. And he's worried about you. And all right, he has a real problem with psychics. Julie, his wife was murdered."

"What!" Julie gasped. She must have been very loud. She was standing in the lobby, but the theater manager frowned at her. "Sorry," she mouthed.

"Yes, she was killed. And under very similar circumstances to those right now. They lived in California. McCoy was already working on the case when Serena was taken from a shopping mall. It was entirely coincidence. This man locked his victims in freezers. And McCoy was desperate so he listened to the psychic they had brought him, and, well, she directed him into the heart of L.A. when Serena was out in the suburbs."

"Oh, God!" Julie breathed.

"I'm sorry. It's awful, but I thought you should know. Maybe you would understand him a little bit better."

"I'm not sure if it matters or not."

"I know that it matters. I've seen him date since then, and I've met some of the women. I haven't seen him care since then. And he does care now. Very much."

"Very much—but maybe not enough. I don't know," Julie said. "But whatever, Brenda, thank you. Thank you very much."

"Of course. Well, you can't possibly enjoy that movie now. Go try, though."

She thanked Brenda again and hung up, feeling numb. She stood in the lobby, leaning against the wall. Okay, so she understood him now. Or at least she understood an awful lot.

She stared blankly at her fingers. All right, so this was hard for him. But it was hard for her, too. She should have run from him the moment she met him. He had been hurt.

Maybe she'd never had to deal with anything quite so horrible, but she'd had her own losses.

She hadn't cared. Her feelings for McCoy had just been too strong.

The movie was letting out. She stood by the phone until Patty came by.

"You are a rotten date, Miss Hatfield! Has anyone ever told you that before?"

"I'm sure they've thought it on occasion," Julie said.

"Well? Did you make your call?"

"Um—it was busy," Julie said. She wasn't ready to talk about the information she had received—not with anyone. She felt too numb.

"Come on—let me get you home," she told Patty. And she feigned a cheerful interest in the movie as they left.

It was late and dark in the mountains by the time she had driven Patty to her home, an old house almost on top of the park area, then driven to her own mountain. She was surprised at how nervous she felt approaching her house. She hadn't thought about the night, or the darkness, or anything but McCoy.

And now...

It was just that the place seemed so dark.

She parked the car and stepped out, staring at the house. Why hadn't she left on more lights?

And why wasn't the dog barking?

Julie bit her lip. Her breath seemed to catch in her throat.

She wasn't alone...

She swallowed the sudden certainty, then tried to decide if someone was outside, near her, watching her.

Or if someone had gotten into the house.

"Rusty!" she called softly.

There was no answer. Only the soft whisper of wind through the trees.

It was suddenly cold, very cold. Was there danger outside?

Julie raced for the house, then paused on the porch. Had she locked the door? She remembered ushering Rusty into the house, but had she locked the door?

Oh, God! She didn't know in which direction she should be running.

All she knew was that she was not alone on her mountain that night.

"Rusty!" she called softly again. She looked down. Her keys were in her hand. Should she open the door or run to her car and drive away as fast as she could?

Could she reach her car?

Suddenly, her front door swung open.

And someone was there. Someone tall and unearthly dark in the night. Someone towering and staring at her and—

A scream tore from her throat, and she turned to run. Too late. A hand shot out and fingers curled around her upper arm like a vise. Another scream ripped from her lips, and she turned, swinging, only to be caught in a set of powerful arms.

"Damnation, Julie, what the hell is the matter with you?"

McCoy. It was McCoy! She gasped, stepping back. Her eyes were adjusting to the darkness. "McCoy!"

"Yes, damn it, it's me."

Relief flooded through her.

"You all right now?"

"Yes, I'm all right now." He released her. She slammed her purse against his arm with all the power she could muster.

"What the hell—"

"You scared me to death!" she gasped.

"I scared you! I came out here and you had left the place wide open!"

"I left it with my attack dog waiting right in the entryway!"

"But you still need to lock your doors!"

"Well, who the hell knew you would just step right into my house?"

"Fool woman, I was trying to make sure that you weren't in trouble somewhere in it!"

"Well, I'm not. I'm just fine, thank you. With no thanks to you. And what are you doing here, anyway? You said that you—you said that you weren't coming back!" Her voice had broken. She was dismayed by the emotion she had betrayed with her words.

Then she felt his eyes on her in the darkness. "No, Julie. You said that I wasn't coming back." He sighed. "And I didn't come back. Not last night. And I didn't mean to come back. Not tonight."

"Then why are you here?"

"I don't know," he said very softly. "Yes, I do. I'm back because I want to go away. With you."

She gasped, stared at him, then brushed past him in a fury. "Oh, no, no, no, no! I will be neurotic by the time you finish with me, McCoy. First you can't seem to live without me, and then you don't want to be anywhere near me. Then you say that you're not coming back—"

"Wait a minute!" The door slammed behind them. Rusty barked at last, wagging his tail.

McCoy caught Julie's shoulders and spun her around to see him. "I will remind you, Miss Hatfield, you were the one who decided that I was not coming back!"

"But I was reading your mind!"

"I do not believe in mind reading!"

"That's right! You don't believe in anything. You don't believe in me, and I don't even know if you really believe in the possibilities of love anymore! I'm trying to understand, and I do understand, and I'm so sorry—"

"So sorry about what?" he exploded suddenly, wrenching her close to him. "What are you talking about?"

"I'm talking about your wife!"

Suddenly, he thrust her away. His eyes narrowed. "Who told you about Serena?"

"Your sister."

"Did she tell you that a wonder woman, the marvel of the state of California, sent me on a wild-goose chase while Serena lay in that freezer, suffocating to death?"

"Yes, she told me."

He exploded with an oath and stared at the ceiling, as tense as a man could be, his hands braced at his hips. "Then have some mercy, Julie! Understand that I don't want to hear anything about what you think you're seeing in any visions!"

"And understand why you want me one day, and not the next, too? I'm sorry, McCoy. I can't. I gave you faith, I gave you everything. I need some of it back."

"Julie, damn you. After what happened, what the hell do you want out of me?"

"I want you to believe in me!"

"Damn you, I don't believe—"

"I know you don't! You don't believe in anything! Maybe you can't believe in anything. And that's why I don't want you back!"

"What are you talking about?" He stepped back and hit the light switch. Julie blinked against the sudden harsh glare. She bit her lower lip.

"Nothing," she said wearily. But she had gone too far, and she knew it. He was going to hound her until she said something to him.

"Julie—"

"All right!" she flared, staring at him. She took a step toward him. "All right, McCoy, so you don't believe in psychics. I do understand. But you don't want anything to do with that part of me. Well, I don't want any part of the disbelieving part of you. Because I really couldn't stand it. A time could come when I'd know you were in danger, serious danger, and you wouldn't listen to me—"

"Wait. Wait right there, Hatfield!" he warned her suddenly. She had advanced on him. Foolish. He was bigger. And now his hands were on her shoulders, and his eyes were silver as they glared hotly into hers. "We went through this once. You asked me if I'd listen to you if you warned me about danger. Even if it was only to humor you."

"Yes," she said.

"And I said that I would."

"You just said that to shut me up!" Julie told him angrily. "So you go right ahead, McCoy! You just keep shutting me out and walking away, because that's the way I want it! I can't take any more."

She was amazed at the emotion that had suddenly risen within her. Her words were hot, impassioned and furious. And there were tears stinging her eyes. She didn't want to see him any more. She spun blindly and headed for the stairs.

"Julie!"

She ignored him and raced to her bedroom. She slammed the door behind her. It didn't deter him in the least. A second later he was behind her, catching her on her bed, flipping her over to meet his eyes when she would have kept her back to him.

"Stop. I know all about Michael Grainger."

Julie gasped, amazed that he knew. Then she wasn't so amazed. There were any number of people whom he might have asked about her.

"Well, if you know—"

"He was killed two days before your wedding, Petty told me. And he was killed because he rode his motorcycle when you warned him not to."

"Yes! Yes!" Julie shouted at him. "And you'd be just like him, telling me that I was wrong all the time. No, you're not just like him. You're worse. You've been hurt once. You won't take any chances. There are no hard and fast guarantees in this life. Not in love, and not for life itself. And, oh, God, McCoy, I really am so sorry. So very sorry. But I do have something. It isn't there all the time. It isn't mechanical. It didn't come with a warranty. It is a gift, and I have to use it when I can. But in my own life, McCoy, I have to have someone willing to believe!"

"Julie..." He started to kiss her forehead.

"No!" she cried out brokenly.

He braced himself against her. Tension knotted throughout him like wire.

Then he gently pulled her into his arms.

"McCoy—"

"Will you listen to me?" he asked softly. "Julie, maybe you could have stopped him from riding the motorcycle. Maybe he would have been killed anyway."

"And maybe he wouldn't have been!" It had been a long time ago. Over five years. But then, she'd known Michael a long time, too. They'd gone to school together. They'd gone to proms together. And they'd grown up feeling the same deep attachment.

The wedding had been planned. Her dress had been bought. The church had been arrayed with half of the flowers.

Then she'd had that awful feeling. The surety of danger. And she'd called him in town and told him not to come out to the house, to wait. And he'd laughed and he'd told her that no one was as good on a bike as he was, and that she was having pre-wedding jitters. He teased that she just wanted to get out of the ceremony.

And he'd hung up on her, telling her he'd see her in just a few minutes.

She'd never seen him alive again.

"Julie..." McCoy whispered softly. He wiped away a tear that had formed at the corner of her eye.

"McCoy."

"Julie, it's wrong to live in constant fear."

"I don't live in fear! And it's insane not to listen to an inner warning—"

"Julie," he interrupted her. Moonlight streamed in through the windows. It lit up the silver of his eyes and fell upon her as he spoke. "Julie, I think that I love you. I can't promise to believe."

"Then—"

"But I can promise to try," he said softly. He cradled her gently against him. "We can both try. And if we can believe in love again, maybe both of us can believe in life again."

Julie looked at him. She felt the brush of his thumb against the dampness of her cheek.

His lips touched hers.

They would try...

And for the moment, it seemed to be enough.

Chapter 10

McCoy looked from the handsome buildings of the Smithsonian Museum that surrounded him on the green of the mall to Julie, stretched out on the grass by his side. Something tugged at his heart, and he realized, almost miraculously, that yes, he really did love her. It was hard not to do so.

She lay flat on the grass at the moment, her blond hair spilled over her, her eyes closed and her face to the sun, the slightest curl of a smile on her lips. He knew why. The sun felt good. The air felt good. Spring air. Not too hot and not too cool.

She loved it. She loved the air, she loved the sun, she loved the white and pink beauty of the cherry blossoms that were bursting in Washington, D.C., today. She had thought his suggestion that they drive into the capital strange, but he had convinced her that a few days away from everything might be a very good idea.

It was another thing that he loved about her. She was so vibrant, so very alive. And she was always willing to listen, to do things, to see another point of view. Against the grass, she was beautiful. Small, delicate, feminine, her facial features so fine. She was wearing a white tailored dress that was perfect for spring, and as she lay on the grass, he suddenly and fiercely wanted to preserve the moment forever. The skirt of the dress had billowed over her. Its soft color lay against the natural earth, the hem just above her knees, her legs bare beneath it. They were bronze against the whiteness of her dress. The outfit shouted of spring. There was a narrow gold belt around her waist, and she wore slim white sandals on her feet. She looked so lovely that he wanted to encompass her in his arms and draw strength from the serenity in her features.

He hadn't wanted to care so deeply for her—he certainly hadn't wanted to fall in love. He hadn't thought that he could ever really love any woman again, not after Serena.

And certainly not Julie McCoy. Not a woman with any kind of psychic abilities. Not when the hurt was sometimes so deep that he would shudder walking down the road when the memories came upon him too strongly.

But somehow, she had managed to dull some of the memories. She wasn't Serena. Maybe there were things about them that were similar. The easy ability to smile. The independence.

The love of life.

The relaxed feeling that had come to him at last while they had prowled through the Museum of Natural History abruptly left him.

He should have stuck like glue with his initial determination to stay far away from Julie Hatfield. He had lost Serena.

And now Julie was threatened.

Her eyes opened and she stared at him thoughtfully. "What's the matter?"

He groaned softly. "Nothing is the matter. Are you determined to try mind reading now, too?"

Julie sat up. "If I could read your mind, McCoy, I wouldn't be asking. You've just suddenly grown so silent. I don't need any special powers to know that something is bothering you."

He hadn't told her yet what the kidnapper had said to him. She knew that the man had called—Patty had told her about the call.

But he didn't want her to know that he was especially worried about her. She thought he had tried to stay away because of her psychic abilities. It wasn't the time to tell her that he had stayed away because he had been afraid.

The kidnapper had watched them together at his house.

Rusty had seemed like the best idea in the world then. Then McCoy determined he would stay as close as possible himself, as well. Between him and Rusty, they had to be able to keep her safe.

Coming into Washington for the weekend had seemed like the best idea yet. There'd been no difficulty with Rusty because McCoy had a town house here. They'd have to be back for Monday morning, but it wasn't more than an hour and a half away, even if the traffic was a little rough.

We are going to enjoy this weekend, he assured himself. They already had. They had both been in the museums on the mall dozens of times. They both still loved them.

"McCoy—"

"There's nothing wrong. I'm just hungry, that's all."

"Want another lemonade?" she asked.

They had just shared one. He shook his head. "No, I want food, real food."

She laughed softly. "Man's food, right? Nothing green, something thick and heavy and really bloody and red, huh?"

"It doesn't have to be really bloody and red—although that doesn't sound bad. And I wouldn't mind eating something green along with it, as long as it's supposed to be green, rather than mold or the like. You got any ideas?"

"Yeah, there's the Associate's Court in the museum. They'll probably have red things and green things. We can run through the Exhibit on Man that we missed after lunch, then we'll have time to move on over to the Museum of the American People, and you can buy me some kind of big slushy float or sundae in the ice-cream parlor. How does that sound?"

"Slushy. Sounds great. Then what?"

"Then we have to head back to your town house. We've left Rusty alone, remember?"

"He's a big dog, he can wait awhile," McCoy said. Then he reflected on the matter. "Actually, though, I don't mind the idea of heading back."

"No?"

"Well, this is supposed to be a lover's retreat, a decadent sort of a weekend."

"Really?" Her eyes were soft. Shimmering. Such a hypnotic color. Green and brown mingling to gold. Just the look in them stirred him, sending wild messages to his mind—and groin.

"Yes, and you're making me feel very decadent. Don't look at me like that. Not unless you want to forget all about the ice-cream."

She laughed softly, and that sound, too, did exciting things to his system. She was so remarkably natural. If he lived to be a hundred, he could never stop wanting her.

If only...

He hesitated, disturbed to discover that he was not at all relaxed anymore. He felt like a caged tiger.

No, he felt as if he had just missed something.

Something was wrong. Or would be wrong.

"McCoy—"

He stood up, drawing her to her feet. "Come on. The evolution of man awaits us—and so does some good, artery-clogging red meat. And then ice-cream. And then decadence. In that order. But only if you quit looking at me like that."

"Culture, McCoy," Julie reminded him.

"They all started with decadence," he assured her. "Every single culture out there!"

With his arm at her waist, he led her around a softball game that had just begun and across the green to the stone steps of the museum.

While they ate, he relaxed again. Julie quizzed him about living in the city. "It's all right," he told her.

Then he mused. "No, it's more than all right. D.C. is fascinating. There's always something going on, good or bad. The air here has a crackle to it, a tension. Almost like New York. But it isn't as big as New York. New York doesn't have the cherry blossoms in spring."

"It's different from California," Julie noted.

He felt the tension winding around his neck again. "It's very different from California," he said aloofly.

She wasn't to be deterred. "You were married a long time."

"Long enough."

"No children?"

"Have you seen any?"

She might have been offended. If she was, she didn't show it. "McCoy, you might well have children that you've never mentioned. Nearly grown, living with a relative of your wife."

"No, I don't have any children."

"Did you want any?"

He shook his head irritably, staring at her. "Am I under an investigation here?"

She shrugged. "Maybe. In a way. You should have children. You like children. I've seen you with your nephew and your niece. You're very good with them."

"Thank you. If I ever need a recommendation, I'll let you know."

She picked up her glass of iced tea and sat back, studying him. Then she spoke very softly, but he sensed the seriousness of her words. "I was under the impression that we were going somewhere with this relationship. I was asking you about things that are rather important to me. Are you sure you wanted me on this trip with you in the first place?" she asked him.

He sighed. "Yes, I want you with me."

"Why? Just because it's hard to have a decadent weekend alone?"

He laughed. "No, I'm sorry, I don't know why I'm so tense. Yes, I like children. I never gave it that much thought. We were young—we both thought we had lots of time. Good enough?"

"It will do for the moment."

"Good. What about you?"

"What about me?"

"Children, Miss Hatfield."

"No, I don't have any. I was never married, McCoy."

"Marriage is not a necessity."

"For me, it is," she said.

"Marry me, Hatfield, and your kids will be McCoys."

"Oh!" she said worriedly.

"I kind of like that," he told her smugly.

"Is that a proposal then?"

He smiled. "Maybe." He leaned forward. "What do you think, Miss Hatfield? Is this spring fever? Opposites attracting? What would your answer be?"

She was smiling. She opened her mouth to reply, but then she fell silent. He watched as a curious darkness seemed to slide over her eyes.

"Julie—?"

"I think that... yes," she murmured. She was distracted, though. Curiously breathless.

"What is it?"

"I think that I..." She paused, shaking her head. "There's something there. Between us."

"Oh, damn it!" he swore. He spoke so loudly that the elderly lady at the table next to theirs looked at him with a condemning frown.

"McCoy!" Julie murmured.

"Julie, I don't want to hear any more of the mumbo-jumbo stuff, please."

"Then what the hell is the matter with you?" she demanded in a heated whisper.

"I don't know what you're talking about!"

"You do! Something is bothering you, really bothering you, and you won't admit it to me."

"Can we forget it for the moment, please? Can we just have one day of peace?"

She looked as if she wanted to argue, but she didn't. She lifted a hand and waved it in the air. "Fine."

He leaned forward. "I like kids, Julie. I'd like to have them with you. Maybe two, a boy and a girl, like my nephew and niece. Or two boys, or two girls—since you don't get to pick them. Is that good enough?"

"Yes, thank you," Julie told him primly. Then she rose, still angry, but a smile curling the corner of her lip. "If you've had enough artery-clogging red meat, let's head on to that exhibit."

"Wait! There's something green left on your plate."

"Where?"

"Oh, no, I'm sorry! It's simply part of the pattern there. Come on, let's go."

Julie nudged him in the ribs with her elbow and they left the dining court behind.

She still felt that he was uncomfortable. She didn't think it was because he was with her, and she didn't think it had anything to do with his initial anger when she had said that something still lay between them.

No...

This was him. He'd been just a little bit distant all day long.

She didn't want to press it, though. At this point, if he wasn't answering her, he wasn't answering her. And on the whole, it had been a wonderful day. It was fun being together. Fun waking together, fun showering together, fun jockeying for a position in front of the one bathroom mirror in the town house, he trying to shave, she grappling with her makeup.

Like playing house...

She did want to marry him, Julie realized. Very much. She wanted to live with him and wake up with him every morning of her life.

She wondered if his thoughts on the subject were as intense as her own. They were walking through the exhibit on the evolution of man and she was giving half her attention to a case that showed skull surgery.

McCoy suddenly caught her arm, and pulled her across the room to another case. The nine months of development of the human fetus were shown in the case, with small exhibits of minute but perfectly formed little bones.

"Look. There's little Hatfield-McCoy at ten weeks," McCoy said. His arms came curling around her waist and he rested his chin on her head. "What do you think?"

"I think it's remarkable," Julie said, studying the tiny skeletons.

"And miraculous," McCoy agreed softly. "Can you believe it? The very idea of just how one goes about creating those little guys has caused all kinds of reactions in my, er, mind. Let's move on to the ice-cream part of the afternoon."

Julie laughed. "We've barely finished lunch."

"Hey, I promised ice-cream, we're having ice-cream. And it's a good walk over. We'll be ready for dessert by the time we get there."

They were ready for it because each became distracted by one exhibit or another. They just made it to the ice-cream shop before it was ready to close. Julie decided on a shake; McCoy ordered a monster sundae, but he did manage to convince her to share in the whipped cream. Then he managed to make a curiously sensual event out of the eating of their ice-cream, even in such a public place. When they left, Julie was laughing and more than ready to return to the decadence part of their weekend.

They drove to the town house and were barely inside the front door before McCoy turned to her, sweeping her into his arms, kissing her fiercely. Julie shrieked with surprise, then pleasure, then fell silent as the aggressive pressure of his lips brought a sweet pounding to her heart and mind and senses. Her hands caressed his cheeks, holding him to her. She delicately traced a finger over the pulse at his throat. His lips raised from hers, and his whisper, insinuative, suggestive, entirely sexy, touched her earlobe. All sorts of delicious sensations came to life within her.

"Damn!" McCoy swore suddenly. His expletive was followed by a loud woof, and as he swung around, Julie began to laugh.

There was Rusty, sitting patiently by McCoy's feet, one paw gently reaching out to scratch at McCoy's beige trousers.

"You're supposed to be man's best friend!" McCoy reminded the dog. "Why the interruptions?"

"Because he's been locked up for hours now," Julie said serenely. She hopped out of McCoy's arms and found Rusty's leash on the entryway sideboard. "Your turn. You give him a little walk."

"Why me?"

"Because I'll make it worth your while," Julie promised cheerfully.

"I'll only be a few minutes," McCoy warned. She smiled and nodded and ushered him out the front door with Rusty. As soon as he was gone she quickly snapped the door shut and raced into the kitchen. She found a bottle of wine cooling on the lowest shelf of the refrigerator, and the cheese and sandwich meat she had packed in the cooler for their trip. Digging through his cabinets, she found a tray and an ice bucket and arranged everything to bring into the bedroom.

The town house was nice. She had liked it from the minute she had seen it. It had an easy flow, with a short hallway leading in from the street, a handsome parlor to the left with a formal dining room behind it, a kitchen straight ahead and two bedrooms to the left. It was laid out well, and the neutral carpeting and tile and drapes were all attractive. It was lacking something, though. As Julie raced through the hallway to the bedroom with her supplies, she realized just what it was.

McCoy had never really made it a home. He had come here after he had lost his wife. Serena had never been here. McCoy had slept here, he had changed his clothing here. He had never made it a home.

Maybe she could make it one.

But that was for the future. Today, she wanted nothing more than to ease the tension that seemed to plague him.

He was always angry with her for the second sight.

But today...

She could have sworn that he sensed something. Something that was very wrong. Something that he couldn't quite see or define, but that bothered him nevertheless.

"I'm going to make sure that your mind is on me when you come back in here!" Julie promised. With that she kicked off her sandals, stripped off her dress and dived onto the bed.

Beyond a doubt, Julie Hatfield had a way with her, McCoy decided. When he returned to the house, he released Rusty from his leash and called to Julie.

"Come this way, McCoy, over them thar hills!" she called back.

He grinned and followed the voice to his bedroom.

His bed had never looked so good.

She was stark naked, stretched out on his sheets on her stomach. She leaned on her elbows, waiting for him, a wineglass held easily, invitingly in her hands. His own glass was on the dresser, and a tray of cheese was at the foot of the bed, embellished with grapes and bite-size pieces of apples and wedges of orange. They were all displayed beautifully.

Not quite as beautifully as Julie.

He walked to her and slipped the wineglass from her hand, then sipped from it. His eyes met hers. "How the hell did our families ever have a feud?" he wondered aloud.

She smiled, coming up on her knees, deftly undoing the buttons of his light, short-sleeved, pin-striped shirt. She nuzzled her face against his chest as she did so, her nose and cheeks so soft against the coarseness of the hair there.

"Oh, I can see where a McCoy might be an argumentative type," she said flatly.

"Oh, yeah?" He set the wineglass down and threaded his fingers gently through her hair, lifting her face to his. He kissed her. Deliberated. Kissed her again. Then spoke softly. "I think I know what the feud must have been over."

Her eyes were nearly closed. "What's that?"

"A McCoy must have ravaged a Hatfield daughter. What do you think?"

"I think that maybe the daughter changed sides afterward," she said innocently, laughter in her eyes. "Then again..."

"Yes?"

"Maybe the Hatfield daughter ravaged the McCoy." With her words, she slipped the cotton shirt from his shoulders. She pressed her lips against his shoulder blades. She teased the flesh with the soft trail of her tongue, then moved her face against his chest again.

Slowly, with a sensuous, circular motion, she moved downward against him. Her fingers moved just beneath the delicate caress of her lips.

She found the buckle to his belt and deftly undid it. His zipper gave to her touch, and she heard the soft groan that left his lips and felt the wild shudder that ripped his body. His hands landed gently on her naked shoulders, but for a moment he let her have her way.

She peeled the trousers and briefs from his hips. She nuzzled him, stroked him, teased him in every manner. Then she felt a second groan, almost a growl, stirring within him, growing within him, suddenly erupting from him, and she was lifted up, crushed into his arms, held against him. Her breasts were pressed against the rugged hardness of his chest, and at the juncture of her thighs, she felt an explosive heat of desire.

In seconds she was aggressively lifted up, only to find herself falling back, McCoy with her. The bed seemed to encompass them. Then quickly, fiercely, he was one with her, and sharp rays of fire seemed to shoot out from the searing center of her to radiate through her limbs and beyond. Her arms wound around him, and she felt the slickness of their bodies touch again and again. She'd never felt him quite so tense, quite so explosive. Muscles knotted and eased beneath her fingertips; drumbeats seemed to throb throughout her, rising to a blinding pitch.

Then the world seemed to explode into tiny fragments of light and dark. She gasped and trembled with the rocking force of magic that touched her.

His arms came more tightly around her. He eased to her side, enveloping her.

And for the first time that day, he seemed to be really at ease, entirely relaxed.

Julie smiled, trailing her fingers over his arm. She leaned her head back. He stroked her hair lightly.

"Was it worth your while?" she teased.

"Entirely," he replied in muffled tones. McCoy closed his eyes. He did feel great. Not only sated, but at peace. And tired. He wanted to hold her now, just hold her, and sleep. Perhaps she felt the same. She didn't speak again. He heard her breathing slow, heard it soften.

"I'll walk the dog whenever you want," he promised lightly.

"Um," she murmured.

Seconds later, he was convinced that she was asleep. He closed his eyes. All the little things that sometimes troubled him were gone. He didn't hear creaks in the flooring or feel a cramping in his leg muscles. He didn't feel anything but good. And relaxed.

"I love you, Julie," he whispered. She didn't hear him. She was already sleeping soundly.

Soon he had drifted off himself.

When the phone began to ring, it sounded like an air-raid siren to him. He bolted up, fumbling for the receiver.

"Hello?"

Beside him, Julie, too, was stirring. She had been deeply, deeply asleep. Her blond hair was a wild, beautiful cascade all around her. Her catlike eyes were unfocused, barely opened. He wanted to reach out and touch her, reassure her. To cradle her against him.

"McCoy, it's Petty," McCoy heard. Then he realized that he was listening to something in the background.

Someone was sobbing...

And it came back, the feeling that had plagued him. It was dread. It slammed against him with the force of a brick wall, and he could barely catch his breath.

"What is it, what's happened?"

"McCoy, you need to get back here right away. He's struck again."

"The kidnapper?"

"Yes." There was a hesitation again. McCoy could still hear the sobbing.

"Petty, damn it, tell me, what has happened? Who—"

"He's taken your niece, Tammy Maitland. Brenda is here with me. She's in pretty bad shape. And the kidnapper says that you'd better get back fast if any of us ever wants to see Tammy again."

Chapter 11

Julie sat on her front porch, alone, and still stunned by what had happened.

And stunned by McCoy's behavior.

She had been nothing short of horrified, her heart as torn as his, when she had learned that Tammy had been kidnapped. She knew the value of time, and she could have been ready to travel with him in a matter of minutes.

Except that he didn't want her with him.

"I'm going now," he had told her, sitting on the side of the bed, pulling on his shoes. "I have friends who can get me back quickly with the chopper. You can bring the Lincoln for me. Drive to your house. When it's over, I'll find you there."

"When it's over? But, McCoy, I can help—"

"No!"

She had never heard the word snapped out more emphatically in her whole life.

"McCoy, I know that bad things have happened to you in the past, but damn it, I can help you. This is your niece! My God, you should be using every possible means—"

"Julie, no, and I mean no! I don't want you in on this! If you get in my way this time, I'll have you arrested."

She'd never been more stunned, and despite the fact that she knew he was emotionally involved and in pain, she struck back, in pain herself. Now she didn't remember all she had called him and told him. He had pushed her away from him and left.

He had taken the dog, and not her.

Julie hadn't wasted any time. McCoy could feel any way he wanted to feel, but if there was anything she could do to help Brenda and Tammy, she was going to do it.

Tears stung her eyes. They'd been so close. It seemed that so many arguments had slid into the past, lost to the incredible warmth and attraction between them.

Lost to love.

But the love hadn't really been there, not deep enough. Not deep enough to sustain them in the face of this crisis. Not when Tammy...

She hadn't driven by the station—she had come straight home. Then she had called in and spoken briefly with Timothy Riker, who had whispered to her that the kidnapper was supposed to be calling in a few hours.

He had waited for McCoy. He would negotiate with McCoy only.

Tammy was out there somewhere. Brenda was hysterical. And McCoy wouldn't let Julie near.

Julie closed her eyes. She had always managed to help through the victim. She knew Tammy Maitland. And Tammy wasn't stupid or foolish—she would never have just gone off with the kidnapper. Unless it was someone she trusted. Or unless she was taken completely off guard.

This was her expertise, she told herself. Even if you can't be there, think. *See* Tammy...

She concentrated very hard. In a minute, she began to see a blurred vision of Brenda Maitland's old farmhouse. She saw the front lawn and the porch. There was another blur, and she saw the back. The barbecue was there, and the big picnic table where they had eaten that night.

And there was Tammy. Yes... she saw Tammy.

The little girl was sitting at the table. Her light hair was drawn back with a blue ribbon. Her blue eyes were focused on a pile of sticks before her. Popsicle sticks. She was busy building something with the pile of sticks and some glue.

A cloud passed overhead. Tammy shivered. She was wearing blue jeans with little bows at the ankles, pink socks, white sneakers, a pink T-shirt and a big crimson pullover sweater. With the cloud passing, the breeze picked up.

Julie could feel it. Feel the breeze. It was cool against her cheeks, but pleasant. It was a soft breeze. A spring breeze.

Taylor came striding out of the woods behind the house. "Could have sworn someone was back there," he said, shaking his head. "Sure wish we had a dog. I heard something."

"You heard a skunk. Or a raccoon," Tammy told her brother. She bit her lower lip, dedicated to the task before her. Taylor snorted and walked toward the house. "Where's Mom?"

"Inside somewhere. Bring me a drink, Taylor, will you?"

"Tammy—"

"Please?"

"Yeah, all right, give me a minute."

Taylor was gone. The cloud overhead moved on. Tammy glued another piece to her Popsicle house.

Then she felt a queer sensation and turned around. The woods were still quiet. She frowned. She quickly forgot the interruption and turned her attention to her project.

She felt it again. An eerie sensation, shooting up her spine. She heard a rustling. She tried to turn to discover what it was.

Too late. She tried to scream as the sudden darkness descended upon her, but something hard and tight was over her mouth. And something harsh and rough had been thrown over her head, like burlap. There was a smell to it, too.

She didn't see anything or anyone. She felt the material, abrasive against her skin. And all her senses seemed to fade away. There was that awful, sickly scent. And the hand outside the burlap, pressing down against her mouth.

Julie suddenly cried out and leaned over. She could feel Tammy's terror, the very last thoughts traveling through her mind. Taylor. Taylor would come. He was bringing her a drink. Mommy would come, Mommy would see that she was missing.

He was going to hurt her. He was going to try to, he was going to try to...

And then nothing.

"Oh, Lord!" Julie whispered. She sat straight up in her chair on the porch.

Tammy, I can touch you, where are you? she wondered desperately.

No answer. Nothing. Nothing at all to help her.

Dear God, was she dead?

No, no, she would feel it. Julie would feel it.

Wake up, Tammy. Please wake up! She prayed silently.

And that was when Brenda Maitland's BMW pulled into her driveway.

Petty had given McCoy his office the moment McCoy made it back. He had been certain that McCoy needed the time to be alone with his sister, and McCoy was grateful.

He had never seen Brenda in such bad shape. His own fear was so rife that it was almost impossible to hold a rein on his panic. He had to. He was the G-man. And he was Tammy's uncle.

But he couldn't begin to deal with the situation until he had dealt with Brenda. And he couldn't even talk rationally with Brenda until he had managed to get her to calm down. She had been sobbing for hours, from what he understood. She had refused any kind of a sedative.

Men had begun combing the grounds as soon as they had discovered that the little girl was missing. It hadn't helped.

Then the call had come. The kidnapper was playing cat and mouse with McCoy. Tammy had been especially selected.

Not Julie, McCoy thought. Because the kidnapper hadn't been able to get to Julie. He was using Tammy to hurt McCoy instead.

McCoy knew Julie must hate him now. But he didn't dare bring her in on it. The kidnapper could make his try for Julie then, and McCoy might well lose them both. No, this time, he had to find Tammy. He had to best the kidnapper; he had to catch him.

It took him ten minutes with Brenda to calm her down enough to utter one comprehensible word. Then he managed at last to get her to agree to a sedative, and Dr. Willoughby, her local physician, managed to give her a shot. "She'll be all right—it will just take the edge off her. She'll be able to help you more," Willoughby told McCoy.

And in a matter of minutes, it had worked. Her eyes swollen and red, Brenda described the day to her brother. Tammy, determined to play outside with her Popsicle sticks. Taylor in the woods. Brenda had come into the kitchen when Taylor had been pouring apple juice into a plastic cup to take outside for his sister.

But Tammy hadn't been there. Tammy had been gone.

"He's got her, McCoy." Tears welled in Brenda's eyes again. "He's got my baby."

"I'll get her back, Brenda. I'll get her back."

"How?"

"He's calling me, Brenda. He wants me. I'll let him have me. We'll get Tammy back."

She stared at him, her eyes glazed. "I want Julie, Robert. I want Julie here. I want her to help."

He stiffened.

"You blame her for what happened before, Robert! You can't do that! She can help me. Please, Robert, she can help me!" Brenda was starting to sob again.

It was then that the phone rang. He gave a quick motion to Patty to see that a trace was started, then he picked up the receiver.

"You know the phone booth, McCoy, and you know the price. I want my money this time. Be there. Seven o'clock tonight."

The line went dead. There was no possibility of a trace.

He swore and slammed the line down. Brenda stared at him hopefully. "It's going to be all right. He wants to meet me. I'll get her back."

But Brenda wasn't falling for it. "I want Julie," she said stubbornly. "You can't hate her—"

"Brenda!" he exclaimed, coming to his knees before his sister. "I don't hate Julie. I don't know—I don't know what powers I believe in, but I promise you, I would try anything in the world for Tammy. It's just that—Brenda, don't you see, we're risking Julie if we bring her in on this. He's called before. He watches Julie."

Brenda didn't care. She knew that her brother liked Julie, really liked her.

But Tammy was at stake. And Brenda was nearly hysterical.

"Robert, Julie will be with you. And Rusty. Nothing will happen to her."

He sighed, looking at his feet.

"Robert, he would have killed that other little girl if it hadn't been for Julie." She paused. "Julie, and you. She had the perceptions, you had the logic. Robert, this is my daughter!" Her voice was rising hysterically.

He knew when he was beaten. "All right. Let's go out and see Julie. I'm sure she's home by now."

"Get Rusty," Brenda said vaguely.

McCoy frowned. He had sent the dog with Timothy Riker to go over every inch of his sister's property. But Brenda wanted the dog.

"Patty, radio Riker about the dog," he said. "He can meet me at Julie's with Rusty. Chief, I'll be back once I've set Brenda up with Julie."

"We'll get the stakeout cars arranged," Petty said wearily.

He had a right to be weary, McCoy thought. It was happening all over again.

Just the same way.

They had saved Tracy Nicholson.

Now they had to save his niece.

But this time, they had to catch the man.

The car had barely come to a halt in front of Julie's place before Brenda leaped out of the passenger's seat. Julie stood, waiting tensely. She saw that McCoy had been driving. Brenda raced toward Julie. McCoy got out more slowly, staring at her. Julie tried not to meet his eyes. It wasn't difficult because Brenda reached her. She needed to be embraced.

"Julie, please. You have to find Tammy."

Julie held Brenda, looking over her shoulder toward McCoy. He was silent, standing there by the car. There was no welcome light in his eyes. He still didn't want her involved.

There was nothing about him to suggest that they had been very close just hours ago.

She squared her shoulders. What happened between them didn't matter anymore. He had said that he would try. He didn't intend to try.

That didn't matter. Tammy mattered.

"We'll find her, Brenda," she said softly, assuringly.

Brenda drew away, staring at Julie, the hope in her tear-stained eyes heart-wrenching. "Julie, she's alive, isn't she? Please, you'd know, wouldn't you, if she weren't. Please, Julie, oh, please—"

"She's alive, Brenda," Julie said. "But she's—" She hesitated. She didn't want to tell Brenda that her daughter had been drugged into unconsciousness. "She's sleeping right now. I know that she's all right, but I'm not quite sure where she is."

Julie expected to hear a sound, some snort of derision, from McCoy. But he didn't say a word. He was dead silent, watching them both.

"Should we go to my house?" Brenda suggested. "Maybe—"

"I don't think that will really help," Julie said. "She was taken through the woods at the back of your place, I'm pretty sure. But she didn't see where she went, so I can't be much of a help there." She stared at McCoy.

"I have to be at the phone booth at the same time tonight," he said tonelessly.

"You'll let me come?"

He shrugged.

"Yes, yes!" Brenda cried. "He'll let you come."

"So what do we do now?" Julie asked.

"We wait," McCoy said flatly. "Brenda, go on in with Julie. I'll have to go into town and see about getting the money. Oh, Timothy Riker will be by with Rusty. I want him with us tonight, too."

"Oh! The money—" Brenda began worriedly.

"I'll take care of it," McCoy said. Julie felt his eyes on her again. "If you'll take care of my sister?" There was just the slightest suggestion of a plea to his voice. Julie nodded. Of course, she would take care of his sister.

McCoy left. Julie led Brenda into the kitchen. She quickly surmised that Brenda had been given some kind of a sedative, so she made her a herbal tea, a warm drink that wouldn't affect the drugs. Then she tried to talk, reassuring her. They sat in the parlor. She managed to get Brenda to lie back on the sofa. Julie wondered if it might not have been better to have Taylor here, too, but Brenda told her that she had taken him to a friend's house because she hadn't wanted him to see her in this kind of a panic.

"But he must be worried sick, too. I shouldn't have left him," Brenda said.

Then to Julie's amazement, Brenda yawned. A few moments later, Brenda's red-rimmed eyes closed. She had dozed off.

Julie was greatly relieved. She tiptoed from Brenda's side and went to sit on the porch again. Sometimes it was best to be alone.

She closed her eyes. She concentrated.

Suddenly, a jolt tore through her. A wild jolt of fear.

Tammy. Tammy was awake now. And she was in darkness.

The panic washed over her like great waves of the ocean. It was a darkness unlike any darkness she had ever seen before. It was horrible. She was trapped in it. It was an enveloping, engulfing, awful darkness.

She raised her arms, trying to fight against it. Her arms hit something hard with a thunk. Oh, it was close, so close. She tried to shift her position. It was all around her. She could barely move.

She'd heard about the other little girl. She'd heard about Tracy.

She was buried alive...

Julie cried out, hearing Tammy's scream echo and echo in her mind.

Oh, Tammy, I'm with you. I'm with you. You're not alone. It seems so very dark, but I'm with you there, I promise. Tammy, I'll be with you.

So dark, so dark, so dark.

I'll be there, Tammy.

I'm scared, I'm so scared. It's so horrible. I can't move. I can hardly breathe.

Tammy, calm down. You have to calm down. You have to lie very still. I'll find you. Oh, Tammy. Your mother loves you so much, so be strong and brave, and we'll find you. Don't panic. I'm here. Close your eyes. Try to rest. Try to dream sweet dreams and don't let yourself be so scared...

"Julie?"

She started, rising up from the ball she had bent herself into, to look into Timothy Riker's young, worried face.

"Timothy!" she gasped.

"Are you all right? I didn't mean to startle you. I've got the dog. McCoy wanted the dog."

"Oh!" Julie exclaimed. Then she laughed nervously. How could she have missed the arrival of Rusty? He was straining at his leash to reach her, panting as if he had just run a mile.

Riker let him go. He bounded toward her, licking her face in one long lash and trying to land his bulk on her lap. "Some well-trained creature you are!" she told Rusty. She smiled at Timothy. "Thanks for bringing him."

"Well, McCoy's right—he could prove to be a big help. We gave him one of the little girl's sweaters and he just about went wild. He barked all over the property, but he lost the scent after the woods in back."

"That's because she was driven away," Julie said.

"Oh," Timothy muttered, a little uneasily. "Well, I'm going to get back now. Petty needs to set us all up for tonight. I imagine McCoy will be back for you right after. Patty is going to stay with Mrs. Maitland."

"That's good," Julie said.

Timothy smiled and waved goodbye and walked to the patrol car. Julie closed her eyes again. She waited. Rusty was licking her hands. She tried to concentrate. Tried to reach Tammy.

She found her. She was still breathing hard. Her little heart was beating wildly. But she was trying. She was saying her prayers. Saying them over and over again.

She was using too much air...

Tammy, don't be afraid. Please don't be afraid. Help me. Try to help me. Did you wake up at all before? What happened? What happened after the yard?

The car. I think I remember a car.

How far did you go? Up a mountain? Down into a valley? Did you see anything? Did you see his face?

There was darkness for a moment. Only darkness. Tammy hadn't seen anything. But she had come in and out of consciousness on the drive.

The drive, I knew the drive. I've done it, exactly the same. You know how you can just feel the way that you're going? I've done it before. I've done it before. So many times. We came someplace that I know really well...

"Julie."

She heard her name. The other voice faded away. She looked up.

McCoy was back. One foot was on the bottom step. He was leaning his elbow on his knee, trying to get her attention. Rusty was barking wildly.

She stared at McCoy, disoriented for a moment. Then she gasped.

"McCoy, I know where she is."

"For the love of God, Julie—"

Julie leaped up, heedless of his heartache and his anger. "Damn you, McCoy, you promised to at least try!"

"We're talking about my niece's life!" he ground out in bitter agony.

"And I can save it!" Julie shouted. "I know where she is!"

He looked at his watch. "Julie, we're just an hour away from the first call at the booth—"

"I can find her in twenty minutes, McCoy!" Julie pleaded. "Give me that. Just give me that."

"Robert! Do what she says. Please!" another voice suddenly begged from behind them. Brenda was up. She was standing in the doorway. Tears streamed down her cheeks silently. She appealed mutely to her brother as they all waited.

"Julie, if we miss this call—"

"Please, believe in me! It won't matter if we miss the call. All we need is Rusty. Please!"

McCoy looked at his sister, then he sighed. "All right, get in the car. Hurry."

Julie raced for the BMW, calling Rusty along with her. Brenda followed.

"Brenda," McCoy began. "Brenda, you shouldn't—"

"We haven't time, Robert. Please!"

Julie knew that listening to her at that moment was against everything he had ever been trained to do. But for once, he didn't argue. He slid into the driver's seat and revved the motor. He gazed at Julie, in the backseat with Rusty, through the rearview mirror. "Where are we going?"

"Your place," she said huskily.

"What?" He seemed so amazed that he might refuse to do what she had asked. "Did Tammy see the kidnapper?" he asked her.

She shook her head. "He came up on her from behind. But he came through the woods and through the yard. He threw something over her head, something scratchy, like burlap. And he had it soaked in—" She hesitated, remembering that Brenda was in the car, turning paler with every word. "He drugged her. He didn't want her fighting or afraid."

Brenda drew in a breath that turned into a ragged sob.

"She's all right, Brenda. I know it. She's just frightened, and trying very hard to be brave. It's all right. We'll reach her."

She met McCoy's eyes in the rearview mirror again.

If they didn't find Tammy all right, he would personally take *her* apart. Piece by piece.

"What makes you think she's at my place?" he demanded.

"Because she knew the drive."

"What do you mean?" he barked.

"She knew the drive. Even drifting in and out of consciousness, she knew the drive. All the curves and turns and climbs were familiar. Something she had done many times. Going from her house to yours. Maybe she even had a peek at something familiar there. I don't exactly know how I know, McCoy, but I do. She's at your house."

She didn't need to argue any longer. They were climbing McCoy's driveway.

He pulled the car to a halt in front of his house. Before the motor had died, Julie threw open the door, letting Rusty bound from the car. She jumped out after him. "Okay, Rusty, you've been working at it all day. Find Tammy now. Find Tammy."

Rusty barked, as if he had understood every single word perfectly. Then he started to run.

He ran in a wide circle.

"Oh, dear Lord..." Brenda wailed.

Then Rusty barked again, and leaped in the air, and started to run.

McCoy was right behind him. Fast. Like a streak.

Julie followed the best she could, with Brenda right behind her. She gritted her teeth. *Tammy, Tammy, we're coming. We're close, we're so close. Just hang on.*

Can't! Can't breathe. It's so stuffy. Julie, help me, help me. Oh, Mommy, I want my mommy, I want my mommy, so scared, so scared...

Tammy, don't fight. Lie still. Breathe slowly, really slowly...

Julie's heart was in her throat. The kidnapper hadn't left Tammy any air. He'd meant her to be dead before Julie and McCoy reached the first phone booth.

"McCoy, hurry!" she called out.

She heard Rusty barking and carrying on something awful. Julie burst into the clearing before her.

Rusty was standing on a mound of uprooted grass and weeds and dirt.

McCoy was beside him, digging through the dirt with his hands.

Julie fell beside him and did the same. A second later, Brenda was with them. They worked furiously.

Then, at last, beneath them, they saw the wood. "Get out of the way," McCoy commanded them both. They jumped away. He found the edge of the wood and began to wrench at it with his bare hands.

Julie had heard that desperation gave men strength.

Now, it did. She heard the boards groan, then snap, broken by his hands. The dirt they had dug up fell into the coffin.

"Tammy!" Brenda screamed. "Oh, Tammy, Tammy, my baby, please, baby, speak to me, oh, Tammy..."

Now it was Brenda who thrust aside her brother. She reached into the coffin, pulling her dirt-laden daughter into her arms. "Tammy, oh, please, oh, please, God—"

Tammy's eyes opened. She stared at her mother. She started to cough and choke, and then she started to cry. She reached out, her arms winding around her mother's neck. "Mommy! Oh, Mommy!"

"Oh, thank God!" Brenda gasped, and then, there in the mound of dirt, she started to cry. "Thank God, thank God, thank God."

"No," McCoy said softly. Julie realized that he was staring at her across the open coffin that had been relieved of his niece's body. "Thank Julie."

Chapter 12

The kettle whistled and Julie roused herself, then hurried into the kitchen to take it from the stove.

She was alone again, but that didn't really matter. Tammy was fine. She'd be going home soon, Julie was certain. She hadn't seemed to have had a scratch on her, but they had taken Tammy to the hospital for observation. They'd probably keep her overnight, and Brenda could sleep in one of the chairs by the bed. Patty had gone to pick up Taylor and take him to the hospital, too.

All was well. McCoy would be with her soon.

She made herself a cup of tea, absently patting Rusty on the head as she did so. McCoy had never explained his feelings to her.

It had been Brenda who had given her the glimpse of the insight. "He's not against you, Julie. Not anymore. He's afraid for you, don't you see?"

At that exact moment she hadn't. But since McCoy had promised to be with her as soon as possible, she did understand. Especially since she had seen the very proud and determined man say, "Thank Julie."

He hadn't wanted to leave her then, but there had been so much confusion. The ambulance arriving, and all the police cars coming. Then Patty had gone off to get Taylor, and everyone had to be called off the search.

Then there was the nagging thought that the kidnapper had not been apprehended.

And the even more frightening thought that he had never, never intended for Tammy to be found. But for tonight, all was well. There might be a long climb ahead. Julie didn't mind the idea of climbing anymore.

He believed in her, she was certain. More importantly, he loved her. He loved her enough to believe in her.

"Hey, Rusty, what is it? Is McCoy back already?" she asked the barking dog. Julie walked to the entryway, taking care to look out the peephole. She didn't want to ruin an emotional homecoming with him yelling about the fact that she hadn't looked through the peephole.

She saw the police car parked on her lawn and breathed out a little sigh of relief. Then someone moved outside and she saw that Joe Silver, still in his uniform, was waiting patiently on the porch.

She started to open the door. If Joe was out there, McCoy had probably sent him for her. He'd probably been delayed and wanted her to come to him.

Rusty kept barking, slamming his weight against the door with such a vehemence that Julie couldn't open it. "Rusty, get down!" she commanded. She caught hold of his collar and managed to open the door. "Hi, Joe. I'm sorry. Rusty, Joe is a good guy. I swear, when a robber comes, Rusty will wind up leading him right to the family jewels. Well, not that I have any family jewels, but you know what I mean."

Joe laughed, stepping in. "Hey, Rusty, you and I are going to get to be friends eventually. Yeah, boy."

Rusty didn't believe him. "I'll just put him in the basement again," Julie said with a sigh. "Come on in," she called over her shoulder. He followed her to the kitchen as she dragged the dog along. "Did McCoy send you?" she asked, shooing Rusty down the stairway at last. He was a heavy dog. She was somewhat distracted when Joe answered her.

"Well, yes, in a way he did."

She closed the basement door and turned to smile at him. "Well, am I supposed to be somewhere? Has he been held up? Have there been any leads? Oh, I forgot! Did he go to the phone booth, did anyone go to the phone booth?"

Joe shook his head, his brown hair slipping just a little over his eye. "I don't think there's anything new. I wasn't on call tonight."

"Oh," Julie said. Rusty was still carrying on in the basement. "What am I going to do with that dog? He can't seem to tell the good guys from the bad!"

The phone starting ringing then, just to add to the confusion. Julie reached for it. "Hello."

"Julie." It was McCoy.

She covered the receiver with her hand. "It's McCoy now," she told Joe. She turned to the phone. "McCoy?"

A shiver went along her spine. The phone was dead.

She turned. Joe had jerked the phone wire from the wall. Her mouth fell slowly open with astonishment.

And then she felt like a fool. A complete fool.

He was of medium height and medium build. His hair was darkish.

Rusty hadn't been confused in the least. Rusty had barked the night Patty and Joe had come over, but when she and Patty had been getting ready to go out, Rusty had been with Patty on the steps, calm, content, his nose on Patty's lap.

"Oh, God," she breathed. "You?"

He nodded. "And you know what, Julie, you are remarkable. I wanted to test McCoy. They always said that he was the best. But I never could get to him. Not with you in the picture. So, Julie, now it's your turn."

Her turn.

He could never quite get to McCoy—because of her.

She couldn't breathe, her heart was racing so horribly. It was all so obvious now. Joe. Right there in the office with them all, watching everything they did, knowing ahead of time what they were going to do.

And no one would ever think that a patrol car racing through the night held evil. No one would have searched his car for clues.

Then there was Patty. Julie had always thought that they made a cute couple, but Patty never wanted an involvement. Even Patty had sensed that there was something not quite right about him. She had worked with him day after day, and she had known... something.

How long had he been among them? Two years? Three years? Long enough to watch, to learn.

And Julie, with all her great powers, had never seen. Rusty had known instantly. While she...

She had to get away from him, that much was simple. If she could stall, McCoy would come.

He took a step toward her. "Come along easily, Julie. I don't want to hurt you."

She started to laugh, and the sound rose. "You just want to kill me, not hurt me."

"You can come peacefully," he told her.

"You know that you are really sick. You can probably be helped if—"

"Now, Julie, I don't want to be psychoanalyzed." He sprang for her suddenly. Her hot tea was sitting on the counter. She threw it in his face.

It was still hot enough to cause him to pause and shriek. She didn't think it would cause him any permanent damage, but maybe it gave her a chance to move.

She sprang for the door, desperate to get Rusty out.

Hell! She had even locked up the dog for the man.

But she fell short of the door because he threw himself against her before she could quite reach it. She fell with a ferocious force, his weight on top of hers. She gasped for breath, swinging and fighting. She managed to gouge his cheek nicely with her nails, and then she started for a second because she saw the lethal fury in his brown eyes.

The eyes of a murderer, unveiled.

"He'll get you!" she shrieked. "He'll get you this time. And he'll kill you. He'll kill you for what you did to his niece. And for what you're doing to me. Don't you see, you will get caught in the end. And if it is McCoy—"

She broke off because Joe Silver was laughing. "If McCoy catches me, he'll take me in. He's a G-man. He'll have to. And who knows? I could plead insanity. You just said that I was crazy. I may get off."

"And you may not."

"Then maybe that will be for the best," he said.

It was the scariest thing Julie had heard yet. He knew he was sick.

He wanted McCoy to catch him.

"Joe, please. You don't want to do this to me," she said desperately, trying a new tactic. "Look, the tea burned your face. You're getting a blister on your cheek. Let me get something for it."

"No good, Julie," he said. His weight was holding her to the floor, his knee in her stomach now, his fingers wound around her wrists, holding them to the floor.

Nearby, Rusty barked and howled. Julie prayed that he might be heard.

Her mountain was quite remote.

He started to shift his weight, trying to grasp both her wrists with one hand. Julie took advantage of the moment, struggling fiercely once again. She tore at his shirt and ripped it from his shoulder.

She paused, gasping.

It was there. The scar that she had seen in her dream. It was just as she had envisioned it, there, cut into his flesh, near his collarbone.

"Yes, I heard that you described the scar," he said distantly. "But I hadn't been out with anyone without a shirt. Not in a long time. And no one was looking at me suspiciously anyway. You're the only one who saw."

Fear swamped her. The awful, dark terror of her dream. The fear that had haunted her ever since. The danger had come. The danger McCoy had tried to keep her from by keeping away from her himself.

You didn't bring the danger, my love. It was there, facing both of us. But, please, come now. Come quickly. Keep me from it...

She lashed out, trying to kick him. She almost dislodged him from her, but he fell hard against her again. Before she could move, he caught her in the jaw with the back of his hand.

She tasted blood. Her head spun. She fought it because she knew she might die.

But Joe was shifting, reaching into his pocket. A handkerchief was stuffed over her face. There was an awful, sickly sweetness to the smell.

He was drugging her. She couldn't be drugged. She had to pretend that she was docile. She couldn't breathe in too much of the drug.

But it was powerful. Despite the strength of her will, a blackness descended over her.

The fight was over.

McCoy drove swiftly into Julie's yard, one of the patrol cars directly behind him.

It hadn't been necessary for him to lose contact with her to know that something was horribly wrong.

And while he had been sitting at the hospital with Brenda, the logic of it all had been building in his mind.

The man had to be someone close. Someone who knew him.

He wasn't that close with anyone here anymore. He'd been away too long. He still had friends, yes, but not anyone who knew his every move.

But the kidnapper knew about him and Julie. And he knew about Brenda, and Tammy, and Taylor. He knew just about every damn thing McCoy did.

A psychic, like Julie?

No, because Julie didn't know everything. What she had was a startling gift.

A gift...that gave life. They would have never reached Tammy without her. He knew that now, beyond the shadow of a doubt.

And it didn't matter. Julie had swept away all of the past for him. She had never questioned the attraction.

She had never questioned him. She had given him her faith from the beginning. She had given him her love.

And thoughts of her were distracting him now. He sighed.

Who...

It had to be someone he knew.

Someone who could ride around easily. Someone with an airtight alibi. Someone who heard his words.

Someone involved with the investigation.

He sat up on the bench, stunned that he hadn't seen it before.

Yes, someone at the station.

Who?

Eliminate the impossibilities...

He rose restlessly and walked to the nurse. "How's my niece doing?"

"Fine, Lieutenant McCoy, just fine. She's sleeping a very natural sleep, and her mother is right by her side. Shall I get her for you?"

"No, no, I'm sure she's fine. If she asks for me, just tell her that I had to go out for a while. I have some things to do, and then I'll be at Julie's."

The nurse nodded, promising to deliver the message.

McCoy left the hospital quickly, feeling as if there were some sort of urgency on him now. He drove to the station. It was open. There was no one in the front office.

There was someone in the chief's office. McCoy looked in. Pettigrew was there, his head clutched between his hands. He looked at McCoy. "There's got to be something we're missing."

McCoy nodded. "I'll be in the outer office."

He sat down at Joe Silver's desk.

Eliminate...

And so he did. Petty—of course not. Patty—no, she was always with him when the kidnapper called. Timothy Riker? No, not Timothy. McCoy squinted, trying to remember. Had Timothy ever been there...

It wasn't right. Timothy just wasn't right.

Damn, I don't work on intuition alone! he told himself. But it wasn't Timothy. And if it wasn't...

Joe Silver. He hadn't been on duty the night they had gone to try to find Tracy Nicholson. But suddenly he had been there. He had been there, at the graveyard, helping him to dig up the little girl.

Then there was Julie's description. A man of medium build, of medium height. Brown hair, probably.

A man with a scar on his left shoulder.

McCoy jerked the desk drawer open. Paper clips, file reports, pencils, pens. He jerked open a bottom drawer. More papers. McCoy rifled through them.

Then he found it. It must have been taken a couple of years ago. There was Joe Silver with a tube in his hand. He was standing near the spot where McCoy and Julie had gone tubing.

He wasn't wearing a shirt, and there, on his left shoulder, was either an imperfection in the film—or a long, jagged scar.

McCoy stood abruptly. He needed proof. But more than that, he needed to know that Julie was safe. He shouldn't have come here without her.

He stuck his head into Petty's office. "Petty."

"Yes."

"You sent someone to the phone booth, right?"

"Of course. I sent Joe. But the phone never rang. Our fellow knew the little girl had been found."

McCoy felt panic growing inside him. "He knew. Right." Then he exploded. "Petty, damn it, it is Silver!"

"What?" To Petty, it was inconceivable.

McCoy didn't have to the time to explain. "I've got to get hold of Julie. I've got to reach her. I'll radio to Timothy for some backup."

He picked up the phone on Silver's desk.

He heard the sound as the phone began to ring at Julie's house. Julie answered. Relief flooded him.

Then she turned away from the phone. "It's McCoy now," he heard her say.

And then the line went dead.

He'd never driven so fast in all his life. The patrol car could scarcely keep up with him.

It was too late anyway. When he burst into the house, he knew that she was gone. The phone line was ripped out of the wall. Julie's teacup was on the floor, shattered. Tea soaked the tile on the kitchen floor.

She had fought. Julie had fought. He hadn't taken her by surprise. She had seen the face of her assailant.

She knew...

But she hadn't known soon enough. If she had, Rusty would never be in the basement, barking in a frenzy. No, she had put the dog in the basement because she had assumed that the man was her friend.

He released Rusty. The dog came rushing out, barking, jumping, swirling his massive body around in circles. McCoy knelt by him, trying to calm him down.

It was hard. He didn't feel very calm himself.

Steady, steady. The word echoed in his head. It had worked out before...

But Julie had been there to help him before. Julie had seen. And now he was alone. She was depending on him, and him alone.

He groaned. "Okay, Rusty, we've got to think. We've got to think."

Patty and Timothy Riker burst into the house behind him. "We've got an all-points bulletin out on

Joe," Patty said quickly. "He's driving around in a station car."

McCoy shook his head. "Not any more, he won't be."

"But where will he be able to get to?" Patty said, trying to reassure him.

It didn't matter to McCoy where Joe Silver could get to—what mattered was Julie.

How much time had he given her?

"Damn, just think of it. You work with a guy every day of your life, and wham!" Timothy said. He cleared his throat. "Where do we begin, lieutenant? What do you want done? Should we start combing these woods?"

McCoy didn't have a chance to answer. Julie's phone began to ring. McCoy automatically began to answer it in the kitchen, then remembered that the cord had been ripped out. He shoved past Timothy, anxious to pick up the parlor extension.

"Hello?"

He knew instantly from the slow breathing that it was Joe Silver.

"Hello, McCoy."

He fought frantically for control. "All right, Silver. We know it's you. I want Julie back. I want her back right now. We can deal with this—"

"When did you know it was me?"

"Not too long ago," McCoy said. He strained hard to listen to the background noise coming over the receiver. He heard a sound that he recognized.

Water. Running water.

He tried to keep talking. "It had to be someone who knew what I was doing all the time. Someone in the station. I thought it was you. Then I saw the picture. I saw your scar."

"And Julie knew about the scar. She discovered it just as you were thinking of it, I imagine."

A wave of fury and fear rose in McCoy. "What did you do to her?"

"What did I do to her? Why, I buried her, of course."

"What do you want? The money—"

"No, it isn't the money."

"Then—"

"You haven't much time to find her. Then you have to find me."

The line went dead. McCoy sat, numbed, staring at the receiver. He gritted his teeth, fighting for reason. There were things that had to be set into motion. They had to start combing the woods. He had to act.

"Riker!" he barked. Timothy was standing before him in seconds, waiting. McCoy told him to get in some emergency help, to get patrol cars on all the main roads in all three states. He wanted more men out—they could be borrowed from any city in the region. Hell, they could borrow them from Texas, it didn't matter, just so long as they got them out. He wanted the area by Brenda's place covered, the area by his own house, and by Julie's. He wanted someone up to the cemetery quickly.

But would any of it do any good? And where did he go himself?

Water. He had heard water. His only clue was water.

Rusty barked. McCoy looked at the dog. "You can find her, can't you? If I can just get you to the right place to start looking!"

It was dark. Dark beyond any darkness she had ever imagined. Darker than any darkness she had touched through others.

And when the drug wore off, the panic was greater and more horrible than anything she had ever dreamed.

A scream rose in her throat, and madness seemed to race through her. She tried to slam against the coffin, she tried to fight the weight of the earth that had been planted over her. She knew what had happened. Exactly what had happened. She had come in and out of consciousness. She had seen, without the ability to do anything. Her eyes had opened, but her limbs had been weighted down. She hadn't been able to move.

He had brought her through the trees, near the water. Briefly, as he carried her, she had been able to look through the trees to the very spot where she had warned McCoy that he would see the black snake—and where the snake had been.

Then she had seen the ground dug up through the trees. She had seen the coarse, makeshift wooden coffin—waiting for her. She had seen the hole in the ground.

McCoy!

She had cried out to him in her mind.

He could not hear her.

Thump, thud, thump. She had heard the dirt falling, falling on the coffin. Then blackness had descended, she had lost consciousness again.

And now...

Now the darkness.

Don't cry out, don't move too much. Breathe slowly, breathe shallowly, preserve your air.

But what good would it do? How would he ever find her? There was so much land to cover, and so little time. And Joe might have buried her anywhere.

McCoy! She thought again. Tears were welling in her eyes. He had finally come to believe in her. And he loved her. Oh, yes, she knew that he loved her. He'd even listen to her. It had all been there, beautiful and glorious. Little things wouldn't have mattered because the love had been so strong. She wouldn't have minded her children being McCoys at all.

Except that now she would never have any children. She would never see the silver sizzle in his eyes again. Feel his hands on her shoulders.

Never argue with him again. Never feud.

Never make up, never make love.

"McCoy!" she whispered the name. She couldn't do it. She couldn't waste her breath. But her mind raced on. Desperately, she reached out with it. McCoy, McCoy, I love you. I love you so very much. Please, you can't let it be the end. You have to find me.

You have to believe...

In the unbelievable.

Think of me. Remember me. Remember the laughter, remember the longing. Remember the picnic on the rocks, and wanting to be home. Remember that you told me I had probably paid the snake to appear.

I love you, McCoy. Touch me.

* * *

Water.

He was halfway out of the house, determined that he'd lead Rusty around Julie's house before trying the forest near his own house when he remembered the sound of the water.

McCoy...

He started. It was almost as if he had heard her whisper his name. God, his mind was playing tricks on him.

Julie! I love you. I can't make it without you. Not this time. Julie...

Think! He commanded himself.

The picture! The picture of Joe Silver at the water, his shoulder bared, the scar visible.

Rusty was running around wildly. Julie hadn't been buried anywhere on her own property.

The picture. Down by the water. Down near the place where they had gone in with their tubes.

His heart was sinking. There was so much ground to cover.

He blinked. He could almost hear her laughter. See her in that sexy black bathing suit that day, her hazel-gold eyes narrowed as she challenged him. There'd be a snake on a rock.

And he'd been amazed. Yes, she knew things.

I love you, McCoy.

He could have sworn that he heard the words. Perhaps he did. Perhaps they echoed in his heart.

"Let's get going," he told Patty and Timothy. "I want to try a place by the water." He told Timothy exactly where. Timothy rolled his eyes, as if assuming that McCoy had lost his mind. "Shouldn't we try his old haunts first, sir? Perhaps the cemetery—"

"No. I know where I'm going. I heard water. I heard the sound of water. And there's a phone booth not twenty feet from the river there. I heard water," he insisted.

But it was more than the sound of the water. Instinct was guiding him.

Instinct, or Julie.

And his love for her.

It didn't matter. They were there at last. "Here!" he shouted to Timothy. "There's the phone booth. Stop here. Rusty, come on, boy, get ready!" He turned to Patty. "I'll take the dog. You get hold of Petty. Get more men out here. We'll have to comb the whole area. Rusty can probably find her, but if not..."

Her air was running out. It was becoming more and more difficult to breathe. She choked and coughed, and then she choked and coughed again because she couldn't take in enough oxygen. The blackness was something imprinted on her mind then.

McCoy, please...

She couldn't think anymore. She couldn't think at all. There was only darkness, and the most horrible sorrow. Just when everything had been so beautiful. She had never imagined that she could love any man the way she loved McCoy. She had never imagined that there could be a man like McCoy.

I love you, she thought. Tears welled in her eyes. Tears that didn't matter in the darkness.

Then she heard the barking.

Her eyes opened in the darkness. She strained for breath.

More and more, the darkness wrapped around her. The barking faded. She was suffocating.

"Rusty! Good boy! You've found her!" McCoy shouted.

He came tearing through the trees into the copse. Rusty was standing over a mound of freshly dug up dirt, barking and carrying on.

"Julie, hang on. Julie, hang on, hang on!" He started digging with his bare hands, shouting, hoping that Timothy could hear him. "Bring the shovel! Get help quickly. Come on!"

He had barely shouted the last words when suddenly a shot burst through the night.

Rusty let out a whimpering cry and fell atop the earth.

McCoy stared at him for a split second in astonishment, then, out of the corner of his eyes, he sensed movement. He fell to the earth. A second shot came bursting through the night—one intended for him.

He leaped to his feet then, slamming against the man behind him. He saw the silver nose of a pistol go flying over his head as the force of his blow dislodged the weapon from his opponent's hand.

But the force of his impetus sent him flying to the ground while his opponent reeled to his feet. Again, McCoy sensed movement.

Then a shovel came slamming down on his shoulder. The blow had been meant for his head, but he had turned just in time to avoid it.

And Joe Silver was there. Still in his uniform. He was covered in dirt, but somehow, he was still the same man he had always been. And he was smiling. Smiling his usual, good-natured smile.

"Missed," he said, raising the shovel to strike again.

McCoy rolled out of the way in the nick of time. He leaped to his feet, watching Joe carefully. "You fool! You can't possibly beat me!"

Joe Silver smiled. "No, you're the big strong G-man. You can beat me. Or you can catch me. But to do either, you let your precious Julie's life slip away. Tick, tick, tick. The seconds slip by. I didn't give her any air at all. I couldn't." He smiled, then swung the shovel again. McCoy ducked just in time, then bounded up.

This time, he caught Joe in a giant bear grip that brought them both crashing down into the trees. He didn't waste a second's time. He looked into the ordinary features of the man, into the face that housed the charming smile.

The man was sick.

He didn't care. Julie was dying. He slugged Joe as hard as he could with a solid right fist. He heard a sickening sound from Silver's jaw. The eyes went glazed as Joe Silver lost consciousness.

Julie...

"Lieutenant McCoy!"

It was Timothy Riker at last with Patty on his heels. They were both carrying shovels. McCoy grabbed a shovel from Timothy and started digging again.

Patty and Timothy were on their knees. Dirt flew.

Hope flared in McCoy's heart. Joe hadn't managed to bury Julie as deeply as he had buried Tracy and Tammy. The earth wasn't packed. Within minutes his shovel slammed against the wood of one of Joe's makeshift coffins.

"Grab it up!" he commanded Timothy. Between them, they brought the coffin to the surface. With the end of the shovel, he wrenched open the lid.

She was there. His Julie. Her eyes were closed. Her face was as pale as snow. Beautiful, ethereal, surrounded by a mist of gold and platinum hair. Her hands were folded over her chest.

"Julie!" he screamed her name. Screamed it loud enough to wake the dead. Screamed it to the heavens. Not again, dear God, not again...

He reached for her. He would give her life. He would give her air from his lungs, and life from his soul. "Julie, please..."

His arms encircled her as he lifted her from the coffin to start CPR.

His lips lowered to hers.

And then...

Her eyes flew open. She inhaled on a ragged gasp and began to cough and choke. He held her up, whispering her name.

"McCoy!" she wheezed it out.

"Julie." He enfolded her against him. He held her there, rocking her with him, smoothing her hair. "It's over, Julie, you're safe." He looked at Timothy. "Get Silver. Cuff him, even if he is unconscious. Bring him to the car."

Timothy nodded. McCoy stood, staggering somewhat with her in his arms. He started walking to the car. Her golden eyes were on his. Her lips were curled into a beautiful smile. Her cheeks were becoming a beautiful blush rose once again.

Thank you, God, thank you, God.

"You were wonderful, McCoy. Just like in the fairy tales. A kiss from a knight in shining armor."

He was choking. "Julie, if I hadn't found you—"

"But you did find me. I was calling to you and calling to you. And you heard me."

"Julie, I didn't hear you."

"In your heart, McCoy. You heard me in your heart. You believed in me."

"Julie, I knew you were near water—"

"McCoy, face it. You have powers of your own."

"Julie," he groaned.

"You loved me. You believed in me. And you believed in yourself. And you found me."

"Rusty found you—" he began. His face clouded over. Julie's arms clutched more tightly around him. "Silver shot Rusty." He turned back. "Timothy, get a move on back there! I want my dog taken to a vet. Maybe there's hope for him."

"Your dog?" Julie said.

He looked at her again. "Our dog."

There were sirens shrilling in the night. An ambulance came shooting in beside the Lincoln, then a patrol car. Petty leaped out, nearly ripped Julie from McCoy's arms, then began a barrage of questions.

"Patty's bringing Silver to the car," McCoy began, but then he frowned, watching as Patty came walking up to them, shaking her head.

"What happened?"

"I—I'm not sure," she murmured. "Silver's dead."

"What?" McCoy demanded.

"No, you didn't kill him, lieutenant. He must have come to. And he raced for the water. But he didn't find a level entry. He threw himself from high ground. He struck a patch of rapids. He's dead."

Julie, held in Petty's fatherly embrace, exhaled on a long, jagged sigh. "It really is over then," she whispered softly.

"Amen," Petty said. "Young lady! Let's get you into this ambulance—"

"No, Julie is coming with me," McCoy said. "Rusty goes in the ambulance. He needs the best vet in town. I'll get Julie to the hospital— Riker, will you please go with my dog?"

"My dog," Julie said.

"Our dog," McCoy reminded her.

A second ambulance had pulled up, and another police car.

Others were there now. Others to deal with the remains of Joe Silver.

Perhaps he had been the most tortured soul, Julie thought. She was still too shaken to know. He had found his peace now, and she wasn't sure that she could help but be glad.

For her, it was over. Resting her head on McCoy's lap, she could only be grateful for life.

She told McCoy that she didn't need to go to the hospital—but he insisted. And once she was there, it was decided that she should stay a night, too. And so she was bathed and poked and tested, and dressed in a clean gown. And a bewildered Brenda came in to see her, and then returned to her daughter. Then McCoy was back, just holding her hand by her bedside.

Within an hour, the phone rang. McCoy took it, and she watched as a boyishly delighted grin appeared on his face as he listened.

He hung up.

"Rusty's going to make it. He'll be in something like a doggy cast for a long while, but he's going to make it. My dog is going to be fine."

"My dog."

"Our dog."

"But he lives with me—"

"Julie, we're going to be married. That means we live together."

She smiled. She wasn't in the mood to argue with him. "Oh." Then she sat up and threw her arms around him. "Oh, McCoy, I love you so much. I didn't mind the idea that I was going to die. I just minded the idea that I was going to die now that you were in my life. But you found me. Oh, McCoy, you had that wonderful power, and you found me."

"Julie, it was logic. I saw the picture—"

"It was instinct."

"Logic."

"Instinct."

"Julie—" McCoy began. Then he smiled slowly. And he looked into her beautiful hazel eyes. "All right, Miss Hatfield. Let's end this feud right now. It was instinct, and it was logic. And . . ." He kissed her lips gently. "It was love."

"Oh, yes!" she whispered agreeably. "Above all, McCoy, it was love!"

And she kissed him in return.

The feud was, indeed, over.

Epilogue

The dream had become her life.

And there was no mistaking the man in the flesh for the haunting lover who had teased her senses for so long.

She knew him, knew him so well. She knew the very handsome curves and contours of his face, knew the silver sizzle of his eyes, the curve of his lips.

And she knew when he came behind her.

Every time...

Because of a subtle, masculine scent. She would know because she would feel him there.

And the warmth would fill her, the tenderness. Yes, she knew him, knew the man, and knew things about him that made her love him.

She knew all the hues within his heart and soul and mind, and those colors were all beautiful, and part of the warmth that touched her.

Tonight...

He stood behind her, and he swept the fall of her hair from her neck, and she felt the wet, hot caress of his lips against her nape.

He held her hair, and his kiss skimmed over her shoulder. She wore something soft and slinky. Something silk. Something that fell from her body, rippling against it, touching her hips and his thighs, then drifting down to a pool on the floor. The fabric was so cool...

And that touch of his lips against her flesh was so very, very hot...

His arms encircled her. She could feel the strength of his naked chest as he pulled her against him. He still wore jeans. She could feel the roughness of the fabric against her tender skin. Even that touch was sensual.

She felt his kiss.

Felt the hungry pressure of his lips forming over her own, firmly, demandingly, causing them to part for the exotic presence of his tongue. Teasing her lips, dancing against them... taunting them, forcing them apart to a new, abandoned pleasure.

And when his lips left her mouth, they touched her throat. Touched the length of it. The soft, slow, sensual stroke of his tongue brushing her flesh. With ripples of silken, liquid fire. She could see his hands, broad, so darkly tanned, upon the paleness of her own skin. His fingers were long, handsomely tapered, calloused, but with neatly clipped nails. Masculine hands. Hands that touched with an exciting expertise. Fingers that stroked with confidence and pleasure.

She allowed her head to fall back, her eyes to close. The sensations to surround her.

The breeze...it was so cool against her naked body. So soft. So unerringly sensual. Perhaps because her body was so hot. Growing fevered. But the air... It touched her where his kiss left off, and both fire and ice seemed to come to her, and dance through her.

She spun in his arms. It was no longer daytime. Shadows were falling, and the breeze was growing cooler.

And his kiss, the tip of his tongue, stroked a slow, searing pattern down the length of her spine. It touched her nape, and the building tempest within her suddenly seemed to engulf her.

And his kiss went lower.

And where his lips touched her, she burned.

And where his lips had lingered earlier, the cool air stroked her with a sensuality all its own.

His kiss lowered. And lowered until he teased the base of her spine. And his hand caressed her naked buttocks and hips, and she was turning in his arms.

She was touching him then. Touching him, knowing the living warmth and fire of him. Feeling the ripple of muscle in his chest. Feeling his hands. Feeling the pulse of his body. Feeling... him.

And he was with her. Her lover, her husband. A part of her. And when he touched her so, when the rhythm of his love brought her soaring so high, the night could seem to be lit with sunlight, and the air was eternally charged with magic.

As always...

When he touched her, the world spun, and split, and lightning seemed to sizzle. And then it came, the moment when the stars burst and the sky seemed to go a glorious gold, and then to blacken again.

As always...

There was the desperate scramble to breathe again, the sheen of perspiration that bathed them both like a lover's dew...

As always...

His arms came around her, warm, tender, inviting. She kissed his hand and lay still, savoring their love, and their life together.

No words came to either of them for the longest time. It was too beautiful. It was spring. They were nearing their first wedding anniversary, and both of them were content to hold one another.

But then McCoy shifted at last. He ran his hand over the growing contour of her stomach.

"You're sure our little McCoy is okay?"

She smiled. "Quite sure."

"Are you sure you don't know what it is?"

"Yes, I do. It's a baby," Julie said solemnly.

He made a face in the darkness. "Is it a boy or a girl?"

She shook her head. "I don't know." She did know. She was convinced it was a boy. But she wasn't going to tell McCoy. He was going to have to be there with her in the delivery room and find out for himself.

"Have you thought more about names?" he asked.

"Yes. If it's a boy, we should call him Hatfield. After all, he'll have McCoy for a last name. He can be Hatfield McCoy."

"Do you really want him growing up with that name?" McCoy rolled to his stomach and stared at her very seriously, as if warning her that their child could fight his way through school because of it. "And what if the baby is a girl?"

"Well, we'll just call her Hatfield, too," Julie told him, very seriously.

"Julie—"

"Then again, I'm fond of Robert. Not a Junior. I like Bobby. When he grows up, he can be a Robert if he wants. Or a McCoy."

He smiled, and kissed her. "Mrs. McCoy, you do know how to flatter your man."

"I try," she said serenely.

"Well, we do have about two months left to decide," he said, and then he sighed. "But we've got to get going now. Brenda expects us there by eight."

"And we really have to be there on time?" Julie asked. She didn't like being late, but it was so nice here tonight. They were living in the town house in Washington most of the time—it was necessary for McCoy's work. And Julie loved roaming the various libraries and archives to find years-old scandals and murder cases for her stories.

But both of them loved to come home. Rusty could run around the mountains. They could both breathe again, really breathe.

They could go anywhere, she thought. Anywhere in the world. This would always be home to them both.

They didn't need to say it. They knew it.

"We can't be late. Brenda is having a surprise anniversary party for us, and if I know it, I'm sure that you do. Petty will be there, and Patty, and Timothy—and from what Brenda said, I think that those two are going to have an announcement of their own."

Julie started to bound up. It wasn't easy with her stomach in the way. McCoy gave her a hand. "Patty and Timothy!" she exclaimed.

There was a teasing light in McCoy's eyes. "You didn't guess?"

"Not for a moment. How wonderful!"

"Yes, I guess so. Anyway, we've got to get going." He pulled her to her feet. "Hop in that shower, ma'am. I'll be right behind you."

He was right behind her. She smiled as the water cascaded over her. Life was really so good. They still argued. Everyone argued.

But she was never afraid anymore. She knew that he was with her, and she knew how deeply he loved her.

Both of them had put to rest the ghosts of their pasts and found something precious and rare. Not many people were so blessed. She had never imagined the danger between them, but they had met it, and the reward had been more than life, it had been this wonderful love.

"Hurry," McCoy warned her later, pulling on his jacket. "You know, I heard that it might get a little chilly tonight. I'll throw our coats in the car, too."

Julie patted powder on her nose. "No, bring the raincoats."

"Julie, there wasn't a cloud in the sky all day long—"

She turned around, smiling sweetly. "Please?"

And McCoy, watching his beautiful imp of a wife—who now, quite admittedly, did resemble a little blond blimp—had to smile.

And shrug.

And kiss her lightly on the lips.

"All right, my love, raincoats it is."

And later that night, when the last of the guests were leaving Brenda's, huddled against the drizzling raindrops, McCoy set his hand into the pitter-patter that was falling down. And he laughed.

His life was incredible. Wonderful, incredible.

And beyond that, it even had special advantages!

* * * * *